GREEN

Terry L. Kennedy

The first of the forsythia is starting to bloom here. The shining faces of the daffodils are popping up unannounced in yards across the city. The mornings are a little warmer, the grass outside my office window turning a slightly darker shade of green. And I know the students will soon be stringing hammocks in what's left of the ancient (at least by today's bulldoze, build, and forget standards) magnolias across the campus.

Twenty-five springs have come and gone since I borrowed my father's old diesel sedan, Betsy, and drove the 300-odd miles from my then-home in Athens, Georgia to Greensboro, a city I'd never been to, had never even heard of until a former teacher recommended I apply to UNCG's creative writing program. I did not realize that I was entering into a lifelong apprenticeship, nor that I signed on that very afternoon I pulled onto College Avenue and Jim Clark, in his Hog's Breath T-shirt and cut-off jeans, met me at the car. That understanding came years later. At the time, I was just trading one formal educational experience for another. I suppose I had some unacknowledged idea as to what I thought might come next—at least where next might play out—but I was so green I had no idea you should carefully consider such things. Looking back, I didn't know a good many things young people know today. I was unaware, for instance, that writers supported themselves doing things besides teaching at universities. I did know that I loved to read—especially poetry. And it seemed like it wouldn't be too hard, with some proper instruction of course, to write publishable poems of my own. I knew literary magazines existed—I had read a couple as assignments—but the idea that I could edit one as a career never crossed my mind.

As I've come to understand it now, the apprentice editor signs on for an education with no defined end point. No one can tell you (no one honest anyway) how long it will take to finish or if success will ever come your way. And by "success," I mean whatever definition or accolade you wish to place there, whether it is a job at *The New Yorker* or publishing a string of relatively unknown authors who go on to win the National Book Award or Pulitzer Prize. My hopes were small in the beginning—simply wanting to read for a literary magazine, for *this* literary magazine. And later, when opportunities presented themselves, I was forced to reassess my desires. I had to figure out if this work was a temporary way to pass the time or whether I wanted to follow its path to some unknown conclusion. And if I wanted something else, what? I had no experience saying that I was fit for the position, but I did have someone who believed in me. And, as it turned out, I eventually came to believe in myself.

I've repeated this story again and again, how I was working for the University of Georgia Libraries and I wanted to learn how to write poetry, *really* write poetry, and so I pulled together a few poems and sent them off to schools across the country—and heard nothing. Until late one April, Jim Clark called me at work and asked if I liked BBQ, if I'd be interested in moving to Greensboro. It's "clean, green, and boring," he said. "Perfect for writers." I've told this story, or parts of it, so often you'd think I'd tire of telling it. But I don't. I don't because of one small detail: I sent my work across the country and heard nothing—until I did. And that one phone call changed my life.

I'm much more aware, now that I'm solidly past the half-century mark, of the inevitability of endings. I'm reminded every time I remember a story Jim Clark told me about Robert Watson, one of *The GR*'s founding editors. Or when I tell my own apprentice editors stories about Jim. I believe each great apprenticeship starts with someone believing in a person before that person believes in themselves. It might start as offhandedly as "Hey, what do you think about this poem?" It might be a temporary job that ends up a career. What happens in between is the important part. The rest of it, what you learn about the work, what you learn about yourself— the apprenticeship—that never really ends.

These days, what I want to do most is read. Discovering that one story, that one poem that really sings is what brings me the most joy, what gives me the most satisfaction. Put another way, I still delight in believing in writers who may not yet believe in themselves. And this is one part of it, this 111th issue of *The Greensboro Review*. I hope you enjoy it.

THE GREENSBORO REVIEW

Spring 2022 Number 111

Editor: Terry L. Kennedy

Associate Editor: Jessie Van Rheenen | *Managing Editor*: Emma Boggs

Fiction Editor: Glenn Bertram | *Poetry Editor*: Samuel Cormac

Assoc. Fiction Editor: Angela Winsor | *Assoc. Poetry Editor*: Cat Robinson

Editorial Assistant: Maddy Porter

Editorial Board: Xhenet Aliu, Stuart Dischell, Holly Goddard Jones,
Derek Palacio, Emilia Phillips

Consulting Senior Editors: Fred Chappell, Julie Funderburk, Lee Zacharias

Continued

THE WITCHING HOUR

Peter Kent

The small cave of your mouth
becomes an air horn. You writhe
in my arms like a snake possessed

by adrenaline and cortisol—chemical
culprits fueling the burning bush of emotion
that animates your small body. It escalates

into head butts—you load your noggin
like a stone in a slingshot and hurl it
at my blue-masked cheek. It surprises us both

that the loose ribbons of muscle in your neck
can marshal such force. Is it possible that,
when the world turns dark, the newest among us

sense ghosts in the room's shadowed corners?
You need sleep. We all need rest. It never ends,
grandson. Though, if you can find an alcove

sheltered from the mind's hurricane, a candle
of memory will always be there to recall how
your heart once beat across the bars of your ribs

in synchronicity with your mother's wellspring
of devotion to keep you safe from the wolves
that inhabit the forest that you now must navigate.

SKEPTICAL ANIMAL
Clancy Tripp

The second time the rat returned, it hadn't even been gone five hours. I was working on my machine, tying a rope around a bowling pin's neck. I planned to adjust the hoisting cord until the pin swung at the correct velocity and height to hit a matchbox car waiting on a wooden slope without bashing anything else. The process was repetitive—tie, drop, pick up pieces, reset—but how else could I get it perfect?

Also, I was sexting Boy #53. My phone buzzed with a photo of his upper thigh. When I first met him on the subway, he'd joked that I only wanted him for his body.

"Guilty," I'd said. "You have such sensual ankles."

So, it wasn't sexting yet, but based on the rate at which the photos moved up his leg plus process of elimination, it would be in three to seven minutes. From the kitchen, I heard a faint but grating gnawing sound.

Mainly I was distressed because it was my fault the rat came back. A website I found, Rats Are Clever Creatures, had highlighter-yellow Comic Sans informing me, "Freaky Fact: Rats can find their way back to the nest from several miles away!" This tidbit was positioned above a *Looney Tunes*-style banner saying, *Rat's all, folks!*

I should've taken the rat farther away the first time I disposed of it, but I didn't want to leave my apartment twice. It was the kind of Hallmark-gorgeous fall day that nature shoves in your face sometimes. The crunchy sidewalk leaves were a jillion unbearable shades of red and orange, more colors than the Paint by Number kits I did as a kid. I spent so many weeks on them that my parents started calling me "little hunchback" and asking if it ever got lonely in the bell tower.

The rat's return complicated things re: the boys I brought over. They'd all ask me the same questions: What is it? How long have you been building it? Why are you building it? How will it end? I'd give my autopilot answers: A Rube Goldberg machine, about ten months, I don't know, I don't know. At that point, I usually hustled whichever boy was over straight into the bedroom without turning on the lights, but now, even that didn't work. My apartment was shadowy and cluttered; occasionally, pools of blue light from the streetlights outside seeped in through the barred windows, glinting off the milky-white marbles set atop their slopes, shining on the ribs of the little metal pails poised to slide down their miniature wires. Only, since the rat was around, I had to keep the lights on because I was petrified it'd skitter over my bare feet.

With the lights on, the boys thought they had license to linger. They'd inspect the pulleys with the worn interest of a retiree docent. They'd crouch by the PVC portion, say, "What's a, uh—"

"Rube Goldberg machine. Chain reaction." I'd point to sections of my project. "A ball rolls through the pipe into a cup, which weighs down the cup, which lands on a seesaw, which flips to release a string, which is attached to a pulley . . . it just keeps going."

By then, I'd be fading fast, so hyper-focused on spotting a flicker of tail or a ripple of grimy fur that when I saw a flutter over by the windows or heard a faint clicking, I'd nearly lose it, but it'd turn out to be the curtains moving in the wind or something. Meanwhile, the boy of the night would mime stumbling into the machine or tunneling his stubby beef-jerky finger through the air teasing, "I'm gonna knock it over!" I'd be exhausted at the mere prospect of having to pretend these men were remotely original in reminding me they had the power to destroy everything I'd built.

I'd say my usual, which was "No touching!" Except, I said it sexy, like a porno prison guard slapping handcuffs shut. Or, what I imagined such a woman would sound like. The porn I watched didn't do plots, and the women definitely didn't speak.

Then, I'd look at the boy hard, trying to recall what about him I could have found attractive in the first place. Without fail, nothing leapt out at me, and I'd know that if I didn't act fast, I'd lose even more interest, and then I'd lose my nerve. I'd grab his belt and tow him toward the bedroom like a sled, but it was inevitable: at some point, we'd both hear it. The rat. Bustling in paper bags or flicking its wormy tail around the baseboards. I'd re-clench my fists, suck in a deep breath, and drag the boy into the bedroom, blinding him with scattershot kisses so he couldn't see the rat and leave before I'd gotten what I'd invited him here for.

I decided to send Boy #53 back a pic of my tits for efficiency's sake. I rearranged my lamps to create three-point lighting and flattering shadows, arguably the most practical use of my art degree yet. Usually, I avoid any evidence I have a body, slug-pink and raw like a fresh scar, but I feel weirdly peaceful after sending nudes. I'm suddenly French-braided, holding a hot chocolate mug with both hands. It's like those olden times people who shut themselves in crates and mailed themselves somewhere far, only I'm doing it piecemeal. Actually, it's more like the ones who climbed into barrels to career over the edge of Niagara Falls.

I mentioned that to a friend once, when I still had them.

She said, "Didn't they die though?"

I mean, yes, they died. Of course they nearly all died. But I can imagine a moment after waving goodbye, clambering inside, inhaling fresh wood, hugging shivering knees, and closing the lid on the world. That moment was maybe kind of nice.

I was unbuttoning my shirt when the rat shot past me like a screeching hockey puck. Truth be told, I was kinda impressed. I'd taken it six subway stops away. I held it inside a trapper cage, which I'd stuffed inside a big, yellow-striped gift box I'd been saving for a special occasion that didn't seem forthcoming. I was so honed in that the rat's every move inside its glittery container was amplified. I felt its scuttling. Every whisker twitch reverberated in my lap.

I only intended to take the rat a stop or two away, but this guy wouldn't stop staring. I'd stared first because he had long, dangling earlobes like he'd taken out gauges, and it inspired me to consider incorporating embroidery hoops into my machine. But he must've thought I was ogling. He, future Boy #53, made a whole show of giving me elevator eyes, all the way up, all the way down. We had the not unfunny exchange re: ankle objectification, and he suggested I join him on a coffee date at the stop after next. God knows why I almost agreed—I don't do coffee, and I certainly don't do dates—but the rat shifted a millimeter and startled me out of my seat. I said I couldn't, that I had an important errand, but I gave him my number.

And now the rat was back. How many miles had its spindly feet traveled to find me? Haunt me? It reminds me of that kids' movie. Since I can't sleep, I've re-watched them all: *Matilda, The Parent Trap,* the one where talking pets embark on a cross-country adventure to reunite with their owner. *Homeward Bound,* it's called. In my favorite scene, these menacing wild dogs try to flirt with Sassy, a Himalayan housecat who takes no shit, and she's like, "Oh, great, *cat*calls."

That line. It makes me so happy. Not because it's funny, but because I imagine the screenwriters banging this script out at 3:00 a.m., absolutely dying laughing at each other's stupid jokes. I bet they collapsed into each other giggling hard enough they struggled to breathe.

Moments like that, and all the movies, actually, make my chest tighten. They never did when I was little; I'm not sure what's changed. All I know is that when the owner, Peter, hugs his dog before leaving him behind and says, "I'm gonna miss you so much," and his golden retriever, Shadow, says, "I know. I know you're sad. I just wish I knew why," I have to pull my comforter over my head, mash my face into the pillows, and slow-breathe until my own stale exhales swaddle me into a half-asleep state.

These quicksand moods overwhelmed me more frequently those days. I thought maybe it was because I kept accidentally walking past the good deli. I didn't mean to, but I looked up while passing it and saw the familiar candy advertisements, sun-faded into newspaper comic tricolor, and the smiley sign saying, *We appreciate your patronage,* and the jangly door I used to walk through. I felt a twinge beneath my breastbone, and I sped on by.

Boy #53 texted again, because I had ignored his text asking to grab dinner.

"IDK," I texted back. "Are you a murderer?"

"Care to find out?" he wrote, which indicated either homicidality or plain horniness. I didn't have enough context yet to know which.

I put my phone down. Picked it up. "Not really a dinner kinda girl . . ."

I tightened the noose around the bowling pin. Swing, miss,

reset, repeat. I tried to stop imagining the rat's toenails scrabbling over delicate sections of my machine, scaring off the boys I did manage to bring back here. My phone pinged, "Pinebox tm? 8:00? [not dinner]."

I knew that bar. Their gimmick was that they were a former casket factory. All the cave-like booths were made of casket wood.

"Casket, coffin, what's the difference?" I asked the bartender once, while out trolling for a Boy #21. I pretended to stir my drink even though he knew perfectly well it was straight gin because he'd poured it.

"Not a lot," he said. "A coffin has a flair outwards at the top, like old vampire movies. A casket doesn't. It's just a rectangle."

I said unless you were Superman-level jacked up top, a coffin was just excess real estate. I told him I enjoy coziness and don't have much muscle mass, so a casket would be perfect for me. He said I was weird as hell, but he was into it, so I should call him when his shift ended. I killed time with a truly underwhelming Boy #21 I met in the bathroom line, then stumbled out of his place at 2:15 a.m. to make the bartender Boy #22. I thought two in one night would feel special in some way, but it was just more of the same.

I sidled around my apartment searching for a clearing with no machine in the background—my tits couldn't take the upstaging—but there wasn't one. I hadn't realized how much of my apartment it had swallowed. The water wheel section commandeered the entirety of the kitchen counter space and was encroaching on the stovetop. Black suspension cords from the unfinished pulley systems hung down, tentacle-like, from the ceiling. I had a mini portrait studio in the corner with a stool and soft, cloud-printed background fabric, but I dismantled it to make space for the particle board that held up the dominoes, tin can pyramids, and glittering paper pinwheels, the most precarious parts.

Maybe it would be good to get out.

"You're a funny one," Boy #53 said, and based on his accompanying hairy knee picture, he was too. Maybe I'd visit Pinebox, for a little while.

I'd gotten the pin to hit its target seventy-five percent of the time, but chance wasn't the same as inevitability. It had to be right every single time. I let the pin go again and it slammed the car's slope so hard the pieces scattered, sliding beneath the couch, where I suspected the rat lived.

I got down on my knees to peer underneath, ready to leap away at any sudden movement. I snaked my hand through the dust, but instead of pulling out a scaffolding chunk, I extracted a glossy pink postcard featuring a beet-faced baby with a pair of silhouetted heads, my college best friend and her husband, bent to kiss its pudgy cheeks. The card had come six months before. I kept meaning to respond, say congratulations, but then too much time had passed and reaching out would've been weird. Except, then I couldn't call to talk in general, because she'd remember I'd never acknowledged her baby's existence, so I ignored her texts altogether. Now we don't speak.

On the card, a stork clutched a banner: *Welcome To The World, Baby!*

I'll never understand how people feel like they belong enough to this earth to be its ambassador. I've been here twenty-eight years and I barely feel welcome myself.

I sat back on my heels, inspected my machine. I couldn't go to Pinebox. There was still so much to do, everything so far from perfect. What if the rat terrorized it while I was gone? I dug my fingertips into my thighs until they whitened.

I texted Boy #53 my address, along with a question: "1:00 a.m.?" I added a purple devil emoji.

When the rat returned a third time, I lured it into the cage with a peanut butter smear, shoved it into the gift box, and took it to Times Square. The place was intolerable—all that jostling and obnoxious wonder. I knelt on the gum-spackled sidewalk. I figured if I let the rat go underneath a hotdog cart, it'd either be so bewildered by the bright lights and big city that it couldn't find its way back, or it'd gorge itself on wiener crumbs until its arteries exploded. I was no killer, but I was okay with being an accessory.

Unfortunately, it reappeared while I was in bed with Boy #56, a cinematographer from work who sulked when I joked that his whole job was pointing a lens in the right direction. He seemed hurt, kept muttering, but then I took my top off and he got over it. We were mid-kiss when I sensed the rat's return. He couldn't hear it, but I knew. The rat and I were basically one. I could feel it rustling even from afar.

After Boy #56 finished and I shooed him away, I crept barefoot into the living room. The calm I felt after sex with strangers lasted for less and less time with each visit. By then, it wore off completely before the door closed behind them.

I focused on the machine's problem section. The ball should've rolled down the ramp and bumped the lip of a suspended pitcher so that it poured into a waiting cup, but I couldn't get the pitcher to pour everything out. I tried fifteen times before I got frustrated and slammed my tools around. I texted the subway guy, Boy #53.

No Repeats was one of my rules—too much possibility they'd get attached—but Boy #53 worked coat check at a gentlemen's club, and who else would be awake at this hour? I granted myself special dispensation.

I described my problem: "Bouncy ball not heavy enough. Tried 15x. V frustrated."

He responded immediately, "Aw, don't despair champ, you'll bounce back."

I snorted and sunk to the floor to draft a response. "For real tho, you a murderer? Kinda want u to be so u can mercy kill me cuz ur pun = v bad."

The rat was back from Times Square in under twelve hours. I barely rolled over upon hearing it root through my trash, just grabbed my phone. My first search yielded an exterminator's site explaining, "Rats are skeptical animals!" I pictured my rat as a tweed-coat-sporting professor complete with tiny pipe, but it just meant rats are good at skirting obstacles. Nothing breaks their patterns from x (food) to y (foraging area) to z (nest).

I had to respect the rat. I went from x (less-good deli, for dinner) to y (machine work) to z (sex with laundromat guy/laundromat guy's roommate/the super of their building). When I ran into the super after leaving the first two guys' apartment, I thought it'd be satisfying, like a game—sex Pokémon, *gotta catch 'em all!*—but it didn't feel like the conquest I'd hoped for. The high wore off before I hit the subway platform, and by then it was late and the LED screen's estimated minutes remaining kept scrolling backward in time and I could only wait and stare at the empty tracks.

When I finally got home, I was tired but not sleepy. I got so wrapped up in taping the hammer to the seesaw that when I glanced up and spotted the rat blinking back at me from the countertop, I jolted backward and hit my head on the couch. I didn't scream, people only scream when we believe someone might hear, but I was shaken up. Being scared without a witness felt strange, like the gesture you would've made with your hands—*The rat was thiiis big!*—got lodged in your body somewhere. I texted Boy #53, "mr. rat is getting v cocky."

Boy #53 suggested I'd failed to put myself in the mind of mr. rat. He proposed I show it the world—had I considered Paris? I said I could never do that to the city of love, and he said he was appalled, clearly I hadn't seen *Ratatouille*, surely the rat possessed innate talents I wasn't recognizing. Boy #53 was funny enough to merit a half-smile, which calmed me enough to set up the peanut butter trap and catch the rat again.

Instead of Paris, I opted for the Botanical Garden. Maybe I just hadn't given the rat a good enough alternative to life with me. When I got there it was early and the gardens were empty. I shot a wedding in the Azalea Garden this summer. The bride was very woo-woo, kept insisting the flowers were "evocative of softness and femininity," which made me gag, but it really was gorgeous, painfully so.

The ground was dewy enough to soak my jeans when I crouched to open the cage. The rat wandered out slowly, like he was equally happy inside the box and outside it. I hovered there until he scurried away into the trees.

The rat took longer to return from the gardens, nearly forty-eight hours, like it appreciated the effort. While it was gone, I got out of hand. Those days are pretty jumbled. There was Boy #56 with the enormous "Be vulnerable" tattoo. I recognized the quote from clips old friends had shared, and told him nothing turned me on like a good, informative TED Talk. He got huffy. He said there was nothing wrong with being earnest and he wouldn't let me make him feel bad.

There was another—Boy #59?—who asked to sleep over, so I yelled, "Keep the change, ya filthy animal!" I was quoting *Home Alone* to soften the blow of kicking him out, but I guess he didn't recognize it.

Then, Boy #60 who yammered about his American citizenship journey and didn't take my hints. He said his visa labeled him as "an alien of extraordinary ability," so I tried to pivot with "Show me your extraordinary abilities, alien."

My jokes were rusty. I was tired. I couldn't stop envisioning the rat toppling my machine. In the end, Boy #60 stood, kissed me lightly on the forehead, and didn't come home with me.

On non-work mornings, I couldn't distinguish the days. It may have been longer than forty-eight hours. It was either two days, or it was nine. I fixated on the pitcher problem. My brain was on laser mode and I was so sleepless and shaky that when the rat returned, I was almost relieved. We had our routine now.

I took him to Asbury Park Beach, reasoning that New Jersey was surely far enough away. I hoped the freezing water might shock me into getting back on track and waking up refreshed for my machine.

But immediately after releasing the rat on the sand, he scampered off in the direction we came from, like he was gonna catch the next train back. I waded in the water but it didn't work. I was inordinately deflated. I couldn't do a single thing right. I considered hiring an exterminator, but I read a Freaky Fact explaining that exterminators don't physically remove rats. They gas your whole place and leave you to clean up the carcasses. The rats rot in the walls around you, turning into shriveled bone sacks, little tumors behind your mirrors. But isn't that the whole point of having someone else there? The prospect that they'll take away the bad and leave you with an empty home in which to start over?

On my return from the beach, I entered the good deli instead of walking past like I should've. I was hungry, but also, I maybe wanted to punish myself. For what, I was not sure. I spent a while running my hands over the crinkly snack packets. Eventually, I grabbed the closest item, took it to the counter, and there he was: the nice deli man.

"She's back!" He calculated my total. "We thought you were dead."

I hadn't seen him since summer, before I stopped coming. I'd been obsessed with this machine step where a knife would jut forward to pop a balloon. It was impossible to get the knife to jab the balloon with the correct force. I spent weeks, months, went through endless balloons. I kept returning because the good deli sold fifty packs and the nice deli man was always there. He started recognizing me, which made me shifty, even though he was only ever kind. It's just so hard to let people know you, like floating atop a sea of stinging jellyfish.

One day, he pointed to the balloons and said, "Gotta beat the heat!"

I wasn't sure what he meant. He gestured out the window at a pair of kids who'd busted off a fire hydrant cap to play in the water. They were six-ish and running, arms pumping, not afraid to want something and show it. The deli man, I realized, thought I was making them into water balloons. I let my gaze linger on the children. The little boy hug-tackled the girl in her frilly one-piece, pulling her down into the water while she screeched and laughed and clawed at him. What would the deli man think if he knew why I really wanted the balloons? That I was doing the same pointless thing over and over, alone? I snatched them from the counter and speed-walked past the hydrant, careful not to get a drop on me, though August was sweltering. And I didn't go back to the good deli. The gap between the life the deli man imagined for me and the one I lived was unbearable.

Leaving the good deli after Asbury Park, I took stock. I was still carrying the cage, I was scatterbrained, and my apartment would be empty when I got home. I squared my shoulders; I'd invite Boy #53 over. Sure, I never saw the Boys more than once, but I figured the rat would come scare him away eventually anyway. Boy #53 negotiated. He agreed to come over only if I'd let him take me to breakfast at the nearby diner. I accepted his terms. Once he got a dose of me, it wouldn't be hard to convince him he didn't want more time in my presence.

When he arrived, I tried waltzing him into the bedroom, but he dawdled in the living room. His eyes tracked the machine's planned path from its start.

He turned toward me. "How does it end?" I was too aware of whatever my face was doing. Was I acting strange? Mean? Needy?

"I don't know," I said.

He nodded at the machine's sprawl. "At this rate, it'll eat you alive."

I frowned, but he was entranced by the machine. "This must've taken you a ton of work."

Making my machine didn't feel like work to me. It was just something I had to do, had to get right.

Moving to show him the pitcher problem, I tripped over the rat cage next to the particle board with unsteady pieces, and though I caught myself quickly, I felt idiotic. I set the bouncy ball atop the incline and we watched it roll down to knock the pitcher. As usual, it poured less than I wanted.

"It's still half-empty," I said, pointing to the partially-tilted pitcher.

"Maybe it's half-full," he said.

"What? No." I looked back and forth, touched the hook the pitcher turned on. "The problem isn't the glass, it's the pitcher, I—" The corners of his lips turned up just a little. "Oh." I raised my hands to my cheeks and they were warm.

Boy #53 squatted by the couch to open his backpack. I warned him, "Oh, I wouldn't. That's the rat's territory."

He shrugged, continued rummaging. "Rats are a part of life. You just gotta get him to pay rent." He found whatever he was searching for and cupped it. "Come here. I have a gift."

I walked over to join him. "Close your eyes and hold out your hands," he said.

I shook my head. "I'm the eyes-open type."

He placed a smooth sphere in my outstretched hands. It was heavy, cool to the touch. I traced my fingertips over its orange surface, turned it slowly. A billiards ball. I sensed his eyes on me, gauging my reaction. He pointed to the thirteen on it. "I brought you bad luck." I opened and closed my mouth like a stupid guppy. He continued, "Maybe it'll be heavy enough for the pitcher."

He half-stepped toward my machine. "Can we try?"

I was unused to people requesting permission. It was easier when they didn't. "It's not that simple, fixing things."

"I'm a patient guy," he said, moving another step nearer to the machine. I took one too. I could swear a few dominoes wobbled.

"It might be unfixable." We moved closer in tandem, marionette limbs tied to the same string. "I know it won't work."

"How do you know if you won't let me try?" Another step. Our footfalls were sure to make the particle board buckle. Collapse.

"You don't think I've tried?" The church nearby began its chiming. The grates over my windows let in slices of sunrise. "It won't work," I said loudly. I only meant to speak over the bells, but it came out several registers too high. It was jarring. He stepped back, I stepped forward. If we were anywhere else, we would've been dancing, hips mere centimeters from the particle board. If he wasn't careful, the board would cave in. The whole machine would come crashing down. I couldn't take that. I just couldn't. I wanted him out of the way. Where was the rat when you needed him most? I quieted my voice and reached for the ball. "It won't work." He stepped back, I stepped—

I couldn't say which happened first. They felt simultaneous. He reached over the cage on top of which I stored the parts I hadn't yet integrated, and at the same time, I pushed him. Hard. He was taller than me and didn't fall, but he stumbled back, his head slamming into the wall. After his shoes squeaked against the hardwood, there was a long, long silence. He didn't break eye contact. He refused to look away as he completed the motion he started, showing me I misjudged the arc of his arm. He set the ball down gently on the cage. It made no sound.

I was suddenly desperate, reaching out for his forearm, "I didn't mean—" and clutching his sleeve, "I thought you were going to—"

He'd meant to leave the ball for me to solve the pitcher problem on my own.

I tried to catch his hand, stop him from leaving, but he moved aside. He spoke to me how you'd speak to a little kid, low, too-calm. He said he was gonna go.

And then he walked out.

That fucking rat. I'd never been angrier at anything in my entire life. I was on my knees behind the couch searching out its nest before the door slammed behind Boy #53. When I found it, I'd destroy it. Dump bleach on the shredded bags and hair strands it curled into at night. Smash it. Leave no home to return to. It was the rat's fault I came back from the beach on edge and visited the good deli. I ran my fingers along the floor trim feeling for holes. It was the rat's fault I had to store the cage there so close, hence the confusion of Boy #53 not threatening the machine like I'd thought. My fingertips' frantic journey around the floor seam returned only dust and splinters.

Standing offered a better vantage point. Seeing the machine in its entirety, I understood how fragile it really was. The slightest wind would decimate the dominoes and a minuscule nudge would spill the water and the tiniest floor tremor would scatter the marbles and the balloon knife could easily slip and any teeth could rip the cardboard tubes to slivers and any bump would warp the strings the buckets rested on and the tracks I laid were unstable toys and the miniature cars were constantly liable to roll away and everything I built could be destroyed so quickly and I knew one thing for certain: I needed to kill that rat.

I called the exterminator. I called nine exterminators. I left messages that made no sense.

"I need somebody who's okay with killing."

"I can't get it far enough away."

"I'm a special case. Don't want somebody ordinary."

"My place has a precious thing; you need to be careful."

"It's urgent."

"Are your guys careful?"

"I need it gone."

"Send me someone careful."

"Somebody help me?"

"Call me back. Call me back. Call me back. Call me back. Call me back. Call me back as soon as you get this message."

I threw my phone down. I had to be practical. My first concern was guaranteeing the machine's safety. Who knew if they'd send somebody careful. I needed to defend it myself. I hustled to the dollar store and bought nineteen plastic laundry baskets. I grunted and sweated hoisting the stack of them upstairs. None of the exterminators had called back. They would soon. I grabbed scissors to cut two sides off each basket to make a protective tunnel covering the machine. My scissors weren't strong enough to saw through plastic. I walked to the hardware store. I came back with scissors strong enough to saw through plastic. I set to work.

I stared at the neon baskets so long my vision warped. The room was uber-bright. Sickly bright. My apartment was covered in the rainbow blind spots you get from staring at a light too long. I slashed the laundry baskets with increasing speed. The washing machine in the basement churned and the old building creaked as it settled and the sirens wailed toward the hospital twenty blocks away: I could hear everything. I felt powerful, like those women who get super-strength when their kids are in danger, who flip trucks barehanded and pry their babies free. My hands pulsed and itched. It was energizing to have a singular purpose. I finished cutting baskets and got to my feet. Now no one could knock over my machine, not the exterminators if they ever called back, not the boys who came over, and certainly not the rat.

I had to hurry. The exterminators would call back soon and my machine had to be safe. I raised a basket a few feet above a domino section and carefully, so carefully, lowered it, creating shelter, then another basket for another area, this time higher, lowering it slower over the pulley part, then another over the seesaw section, the safe structure covering most by now, another basket shielding the machine, though I had to speed up before the exterminators arrived, so I put down another basket, was almost done, placed another basket, covered another section, one more basket, another, I grabbed the second-to-last basket and held it tight in my hands ready to cover the pitcher problem which, yes, the pool ball seemed like it'd solve when I had the time for testing and I lowered it bit by bit over the machine and then—

And then, such a little thing, the basket's jagged edge brushed

a marble on the way down. And the machine started to fall. The
dominoes chased each other. The levers flipped. The hatches
swung closed. The seesaws clattered. The machine had been hit in
the center, so it fell in two directions, from the inside out, like two
velvet curtains. The pitcher poured and halfway filled the cup.
The bouncy balls hurtled down their slopes and pinged off the
walls. The miniature cars rolled away. The knife lunged blindly.
The pulleys released. It was all over in a minute.

I sat surrounded by my shattered machine and waited for the rat.
It took hours to come back. The sky darkened outside, then got
light again. My sit bones went numb. I tried counting how many
days it'd been since I'd slept. I wanted the rat to come back so I
could kill it for good. Also, I thought I might be lonely.

When the rat returned, it slipped under the door like its bones
were liquified and, once inside, cocked its head at me. It walked
right into the cage. I hadn't even set the peanut butter trap. I
stuffed the cage in the gift box and took the subway to Pier 11
on Wall Street. There was a ferry that looped between the docks
and IKEA, and it was free on weekends. I stood waiting to board
the ferry, clasping the box to my chest. Inside, the rat was still. I
shuffled forward with the line.

My plan was to leave the rat in IKEA. It needed a real home,
and maybe somewhere in that legion of cushions and curtains and
lights it could find one. But edging closer to the ferry's entrance,
trying not to bump into anybody, I realized the stupidity of my
idea. It was futile. The rat would just keep coming back. If I
wanted it gone, I'd have to kill it myself.

We boarded the ferry and I headed for the outside deck portion
even though it was freezing and the water smelled putrid and the
wind whipped my hair in my eyes and it stung. I perched the box
on the railing for inspection. All the glitter had rubbed off in the
course of my many trips. The once-crisp edges had worn down,
exposing the pulpy cardboard underneath. It was covered in dings
and scratches.

A loudspeaker announcement crackled. I turned to face the
direction the voice came from, though the speaker was clearly
inside. I could see him through the tinted window. A skinny guy

with pockmarked skin and an utter lack of interest in his own spiel.

"Floatation devices are stored and available for your safety," he said, pointing lazily at the windows where it was clear the floatation devices were not stored. I stared at his curly hair, the way he shifted from foot to foot. If I wanted to, I could've taken him home with me. It wouldn't have taken much. I could've made a joke about life jackets and needing somebody to save me. Mouth-to-mouth. Etc. I watched the idle flex of his jaw as he ran through safety policies. I could've fucked him. It would've been easy. I turned my back on the cabin and looked out over the water.

The metal railing had triangle patterns. I hooked my pinky around a vertex. It reminded me of something someone, Boy #14 or #32, maybe, once said. I was describing a house of cards I saw in a store window, how it stressed me out. If I were going to make one, I said, I'd tape the apexes together for a stable hinge.

Whoever it was, he laughed so hard that little spittle projectiles flew from his mouth. He kept choking with each inhale until he finally got out the words: "That doesn't count."

I wanted to know why. He was laughing, but I was dead serious.

By then he was pounding his fist on the bar like a cartoon character. "Because the whole point is that it might fall."

I looked around the ferry. Inside its cage, the rat wriggled a little, causing the box to bump gently against my arm. The only others outside in the weather with me were a little boy and his shih tzu. He had a package of green votive candles, probably something his parents hoped to return, and he was rolling them across the deck for the dog to chase. The boy pitched candles left, right. The dog pounced again and again, wild, thrilled. I felt the rat nuzzling the box's inside corners. The candles the dog had already caught and abandoned littered the deck like lily pads.

The ferry trundled toward the docks where customers stood laden with hefty blue bags and creased mouths. The bored guy got back on the speakers to drone instructions for safe disembarkation. The water below was choppy and gray and seemed so far away. The other passengers shouldered their bags and trudged toward the ferry doors. The deck where I stood was nearly deserted now and the cabin was rapidly emptying. The metal railing was cold against my forearms. I had never been good at getting rid of things.

I felt something wet and looked down to see the dog nosing my ankles. It looked up at me and its smushed face was ugly-charming, like a snooty little Persian cat.

The cat in *Stuart Little* has a similar face. I just re-watched it. The Persian initially hates that Stuart is his master, but near the movie's end he comes around. He even saves Stuart when he's threatened by some cats perched in a tree overhanging a lake. He breaks off the branch holding the rival cats and they plummet, yelping, into the water.

"Just doggy-paddle!" an enemy cat calls to one of his comrades.

"*Doggy*-paddle?" the other cat cries. "I'd rather drown!"

What a stupid line. I love it so much. I bet the screenwriters who thought it up pissed themselves laughing, that they play-punched each other over such a complete eye-roller. Maybe one held the script in the air and yelled, "I went to film school for *this*?" and everybody fell out of their chairs laughing. Imagining it made my eyes well up, it made it hard to swallow, it made me start to cry.

UNSAVAGE THE BOY

Nicole Adabunu

after ansel elkins

unhook his gaze
from hers   unappetite the lust
burning in his belly   dislocate
the heat of his heavy limbs
unpin his shadow from her
silhouette   peel his prickly pubic
from under her hip   undress
her skin, the stench of his salt   unglisten
his sweat from her eye   unclot
her cold blood on the bed sheet
and send it back to the heart.   unfasten
his fingers from her esophagus   return
every choked vein that screamed
against his grasp, return every silent swallow
to her throat, return every stop he pushed
into her pulse, return every stop
his ears neglected every no
every please she begged like a prayer
under him   return the blood

bleach the bed sheet back
to white   repaint the night
a kinder color   uncolor
the memory from her mind
return the girl her sanity
return the boy's hands
to his sides   return the boy
to his mother   return the sin
back to god   return the sin back
to god

CATALOGING

Natalia Conte

These days I'm scared of almost everything.
      Trees that look like men. Men that look

like trees. The status of honeybees, round
      bodies dizzy on sweet. They don't know

how quickly the hum of their hive will begin
      to fade. How larger beasts come to rip away.

Today, I've swallowed a baby bird
      and it flaps against my insides trying

to loose its wings. Tomorrow,
      I'll swallow a stick of dynamite

and it will pulse, almost alive,
      under the stomach skin. I hold

each squirrel closest to my heart: they fiddle
      with the atrium, knock on each valve

as if searching for something buried. My chest:
      a stubborn acorn refusing release. Give me some

of my body back. I can't hold
      all of these creatures in my hollows

for long. I watch girls in their patterned leggings
      stuff ducks full of white bread,

think of the way their wings will mutate
      to look like angels, useless in the jaws

of a badger. Uncovered faces, everywhere.
            The persistence of summer and shorts.

Why is it in our nature to think of joy
            and fear as two separate wings

not connected by the same hallway?
            There are nice things too, right now,

always. The imagined sound of the whole world
            breathing in unison. The nuzzle of a cat scalp

against my open palm. The way I always take
            a small offering and think of it as more.

Even here, the light cuts my bedroom into sections,
            makes each lovely in its multiplicity.

THE MAVROVO GHOST HOTEL WELCOMES ALL

Ellen Rhudy

More tourists were coming now, and from less familiar places: Their cars bore plates from Slovenia, Estonia, Turkey. They spoke languages Goran didn't understand. Their buses had dredged a bare patch in the grass. They stayed in the new Mavrovo Ghost Hotel, just in view of the drowned church which was now the village's greatest attraction. Often Goran caught the tourists staring at him, taking photographs as he sat at the café or walked his neighbor's cow to its field. He liked their disappointment when they glanced at their phone screens to find what he could have told them to expect: nothing, a dusty street without cow or man. The recorded world rarely matched the world people thought they knew, and every day he saw the same defeat registering on visitors' faces.

Now, though, he bore his own defeat: that Bojan would not be coming home. How many years had it been since his son moved his family from Gostivar to Staten Island, a city that was removed both by an ocean and an entire world? Goran had no real sense for time—hours and days, punctuality, all of that belonged to the living. Still, he felt a pressure around his son's absence, the malformed thought that if he didn't come this year he might never come. "Write him back," he told his wife, Rosa. "Tell him we need him."

"Need him for what?" asked Rosa. "Why don't you write him, if it's that important?"

"Because I always write him. Now it's your turn." None of this was true, but Goran stated it with the confidence of fact. He watched over Rosa's shoulder as she composed her message and held it up for him to see.

The girls need to see their home. Next summer they can go to songwriting camp. Tell them we love them. We have a camp here.

"We do?" Goran asked as she hit send.

"Some type of ghost camp," Rosa said. "Something the hotel is putting on." As she spoke, Goran imagined children dressed in bedsheets, shouting spooky stories as they ran through the woods. Maybe it would be enough to draw Bojan home, and when he arrived the camp would be forgotten. There would only be family evenings eating around the same table, sitting lakeside and watching the church's shadow gloam across the water, tossing items for the satisfaction of watching Goran's dog, Metchka, carry them back. "Find a brochure when you're out," she said, giving Goran the sense that he was already on his way—to where, he didn't know. They would photograph the brochure for Bojan.

First he went where he always went, to Sasho's café. In the hotel's opening year Sasho had identified the potential for new business and erected signs advertising specials on Skopsko beer, or a discounted rate coffee with accompanying pastry. These signs still lilted, half-strung, from the ceiling, but there were no pastries and only locals present. "Worse than leeches," Sasho liked to say of the tourists. He said it now as these interlopers sat before the café with sandwiches from the hotel kitchen, and bottles of Pelisterka water carried in from the capital. Scattering garbage but no money across the village while Goran sipped his bitter macchiato and smudged cigarettes into the overflowing plastic ashtray. This another relic of Sasho's more enterprising days, with little Caspers imprinted on its side.

"So what's new," Goran asked as a tourist retrieved a butt from the ashtray. "They take, they take, they take," he mouthed to Sasho.

"Look at that!" the woman exclaimed. "They can still impact the physical world—look!"

Goran watched how she held the cigarette butt like a religious relic. He sighed. He wanted one person, only, to consider his garbage as nothing more than garbage. "You know about this camp?" he asked Sasho. "Bojan and Snezhana might bring the girls."

"Really? You want your own grandchildren involved in all that?"

"No," said Goran. The hotel had ruined his business and the remnants of his life contained therein. Even revising his home-share listing to match the latest marketing (*Ghost house, sleep alongside a real ghost, eat ghost food prepared by a ghost*) hadn't resulted in new business. No, he didn't want anything to do with the hotel. "But it's different for our children," he said. "They like those things. Maybe they bring the grandchildren back for this stupid camp and then they remember what we have here, they don't have to go."

"You think that's likely?" By the tone of his voice, Sasho did not. He prepared another coffee for Goran, banging more than necessary, and carried his own drink over to join him. "Photos aren't free!" he shouted at the tourists, but neither man stood to extract the piddling, reluctant denars that might be offered in exchange for the blank spaces standing in lieu of their images.

Goran stirred a packet of sugar into his coffee and licked the plastic spoon, half the size of his pinky nail. Most of the tourists faced the same way as him, gazing across the water and waiting for the two children—Goran's brother Dushko, and his childhood friend Ljuba—to make an appearance in the drowned church. For half the year the church loomed beneath the lake with only its bell tower visible. Now that it was summer, the dam drawn low, it stood on a muddy hump. Indecipherable green plants straggled from its gaping windows. Occasionally, Dushko and Ljuba could be glimpsed in its blackened interior, where they spent their days in the calm repose unique to drowning victims.

The two of them were, Goran thought, the last memories of what the village had once been, before it was flooded, before its homes were rebuilt on the new shores. Goran had been too young to remember the day the pair of them skated across the too-thin ice of the new lake. That Dushko was his brother was something he knew mostly because it had been so frequently recited at him. Still, he considered their dripping footprints and mildewed scarves a reminder of something the tourists wouldn't ever understand— something he could access, and they could never hope to.

It was evening when Goran remembered the brochure as not just an idea but an object he had to procure. Toše had come down from the stilted park service building on the main road, and there went most of the day—because Toše always had the latest gossip on construction and major touristic incursions, his latest rumor being that a group from Japan would be bussing through any day. Japan! Something in that distance delighted Goran, and he thought he would like to photograph the tourists in return; he would ask Rosa where the camera's charging cable was.

The tourists—the ones who didn't interest him as the theoretical dozens of Japanese men and women did—stood at water's edge, still staring at the church which had half-vanished into the ashing night. Goran dragged on his cigarette as he walked by these people so insultingly full of life. While he had been slouched in the café, they had been hiking and riding horses. They had taken excursions that he could have narrated better than their big city tour guides dressed in white rags and powdered faces. These hordes hadn't been the types he'd wanted to attract years earlier when he coaxed the other villagers into developing their tourism. Maybe the type of tourist he wanted didn't exist, though: someone who would look at his home with appreciation rather than judgement. Or without fear—a wish that occurred to him when he spat next to a woman's hiking boot and raised her scream.

"He's coming for me!" she shrieked, stumbling back and nearly dropping her camera with its expensive lens. "The ghost!"

A laughable accusation. "I'm not—" Goran began, but no one heard. Cameras clattered and the woman described her close encounter for the gathered tourists. The ghost had approached her—he had reached his chain-wrapped arm to her—and when she drew back, that was when he had spit. She pointed to her boot, to the faint globular stain that was, apparently, the only mark Goran could hope to leave on this world. He continued toward the hotel while they were distracted by their storytelling.

The building was white, four stories, with a grand deck overlooking the lake. Goran had once imagined its land as a ski lodge, until the day he woke to the low-grade hum of construction equipment and the discovery that some stranger from Skopje had staked his claim on the better part of the village. The newspapers reported the construction as a revitalizing investment, awaited ever since the avalantial tragedy that had smothered a dozen electricians working on the new power plant before carrying a wave of snow, rocks, trees, and mud to the church's back and no farther—a miracle if Goran had ever seen one. The villagers rarely ventured inside the hotel; it was so clearly not a place for them. No one had been in since Toše had applied to be a waiter and been turned away for lacking the proper, or any, employment paperwork. Goran rested his hand for a moment on the gold-plated door handle before pushing inside.

A woman sat behind a wooden desk, her hair lank on either side of her face. Scratching her nose, her sleeve shifted to reveal the line where her makeup ended and the flush of skin began. Her eyes were rimmed in black, her lips a deep red. That's not what a ghost looks like, Goran wanted to tell her. Real ghosts look just like people.

He suspected the costumes and makeup were meant as a comfort to the guests. You are alive, the white-painted faces said. You will know if you become a ghost, you will never become a ghost. The girl looked straight through him as he approached. She blinked three slow blinks—that was how she thought dead people blinked, as if they had forgotten the use of their own muscles.

"Can I take some information on your summer camp?" he asked.

Her mouth drifted open. For a moment he thought she was seeking an answer. Then a scream spiraled from her, ricocheting through the marble entryway. Here came the beating of feet as guests ran to see what had happened, emerging from their rooms and the dining hall and all the building's other hidden places.

Goran took a handful of brochures from the desk. He had only asked to be polite. The brochures were right there for anyone to take. But his fistful of papers was another upset; the woman burst into racketing sobs, the tourists and other false ghosts gathering around her as Goran backed away. "They won't be forgotten!" the receptionist screamed, pointing to him. Cameras, cameras. "They'll never let us rest!"

He shoved through the door, past the crowds, through the village. "They're crazy," he told Rosa when he gave her the half-dozen brochures. "You can't let our grandchildren go to that camp. There's no reasoning with them."

"Calm down." Where she found her reserves of ease, he could never guess, only sometimes he longed for her to share the secret with him. "You don't think our grandchildren would be taken in by those types?" Besides, she told him, she had made his favorite, tavche gravche, for dinner—and Toše had been by and left a new superhero movie, with Serbian subtitles—and Ljuba and Dushko were there, in the corner, a damp circle spreading from their feet as they trained their wanting eyes on Goran.

Something in the dead children had been changing. It was hard to say what, exactly, but Goran found he was again unable to shake the sense of their alterations. He glanced up at them every bite or two until even Rosa noticed and stopped watching her soap opera long enough to ask what had gotten into him.

"Nothing," Goran said, and tried to make his gaze a more casual thing. The children reminded him, though, of his more corporeal days, when he might feel an ache in his jaw and the accompanying need to press his index finger to the pain every few minutes to check its continuing presence. By the end of the day his jaw would hurt worse from the attention, and he would wonder if the pain had even been real to start with, or if it was only the result of his persistent attention. Stop looking, he told himself, because his gaze would only make more to look at; but no denying there was something in their eyes, which had once been blank as black buttons. They discomfited him in a way they never had, and he wondered briefly if he was beginning to see something in them that Rosa had always sensed. She'd never liked the children in their house, always claiming they left water puddles or vague and indestructible odors. Goran had only ever seen them with pity, and sometimes confusion and wonder—why had they been maintained in a form so different from his own?

"You want to watch the movie?" Rosa asked when her credits rolled.

While she collected their plates, Goran used a sleeve to clean the DVD's glossy underbelly, then slid it into the player. He felt the children's gaze on his back. The pair of them had never been apart, not since that day the ice shattered beneath them. A stupid accident. "You don't want something to eat?" he whispered, glancing back, though they never did. It was their stillness that unnerved. If only they would move. He hunched on the sofa and found his way through the movie's menu, never a predictable route to be found on Toše's pirated editions—no telling what button would do what—before Rosa returned with a plate of cookies.

"I sent a picture of the brochure," she said. She folded her legs beneath her.

Goran did the math. It would be two o'clock on Staten Island. Maybe Bojan would glance at the message; in four hours he would be home from work, maybe a few minutes to discuss the matter with his wife. Goran and Rosa should have their answer when they woke in the morning. Despite his calculations, he listened for the phone's exclamation after starting the movie and kept glancing at the children dripping in their corner. Within minutes he lost the movie's thread, some search for a magic stone. (Would it confer additional powers on the superheroes?) He was unsure what was wrong with him. The superheroes recovered the stone, and unleashed further rounds of mayhem.

The morning brought no answer. In Goran's memory, Bojan had been such an attentive boy, always sitting with his hands folded and a book on his lap, ready to leap to action when Goran suggested some chore or adventure. When had this changed? "Send him another message," Goran said. "Maybe he didn't get the picture. Sometimes if the file's too big—"

"You message him," said Rosa.

Goran walked to the front stoop, where he knelt to lace his boots. "He won't listen to me," he said, tying. "It's only you whose voice matters anymore. Tell him Metchka misses him." At her name, the dog appeared at his knee, nudging his hand. She was so large he had once allowed the neighboring children to ride her like a good-natured pony. His own grandchildren had never had this privilege. "He'll listen to you," he repeated before he and Metchka left the house. "Remind him how he loves his mother."

The only thing Goran knew about ghosts was that they were left on Earth for a mission. Perhaps they had been cruelly murdered and would lead the police to their killer, or they would assist other ghosts in coming to terms with their own ghostliness, its causes and meanings. For himself, Goran had no real sense of mission and only wished to know what it would be like to move through the afterlife with intention. He walked with Metchka to the lake and they stood there, well-distanced from the tourists, watching the church. It was uncomfortable to find himself always in this shared position, all of them waiting—to no apparent purpose—

for the children to arrive.

Goran was tossing pebbles across the water, mostly failing to skitter them over the surface, when the tourists' murmurations rose. With Metchka, he walked closer; this further increased their excitement. "—at odds," said one man, and another glanced at Goran and whispered to her husband that "The ghosts don't welcome them."

"Who isn't welcome?" Goran asked. "What's at odds?"

The water padded against the shore. Metchka walked to the café, leaving a trail of wet prints.

"The children," said one of the men. He stood too straight, as if someone had just slapped the small of his back and startled him to attention. "The ones you fight with."

"Who told you that?" Goran asked. Now the ramrod man receded. "Who am I fighting?" Again, no answer. Some reenactor at the hotel had devised this, he thought, a flashy falsity to add some fun to dull Mavrovo. He followed Metchka to Sasho's but kept wondering at the story as he drank his coffee and smoked his cigarettes and dug his fingers into the soft fold beneath Metchka's right ear. "You haven't heard this?" he asked Sasho. Metchka pressed her head against his knee as he worked out the old itch for her.

"Some new thing from the hotel." Sasho sat with Goran, patted Metchka's head. Her tail thumped a wavering cloud of dust into life.

"New since yesterday?"

"It's like a fire. It's little, it's little, and then—a flash—it's everywhere."

Goran sighed. Was this how fire spread? "Why would we fight with Ljuba and Dushko?"

"Oh, they have it all worked out." Sasho leaned forward, elbows propped on the table. He was excited. "We—all of us here, in Mavrovo—see the church as our rightful property. But as long as Dushko and Ljuba are there, we can't set foot on the church grounds. It's consecrated. Thus, we are at war with them. Forever, and for all times, and—"

"Makes no sense." Goran rested his cigarette on the ashtray. "They see the children come in the village, don't they?"

Sasho waved his hand. "And they'll come up with another story. It's just to get them a little excited and spread word for their camp. No harm done."

Goran watched the ash progressing along his cigarette until the whole was extinguished. Was it harmless? He recalled how those women had screamed at him yesterday. In the early days of the hotel he had been treated as nothing more than local color. A laughable and bumbling figure, not a conception he liked but one he could live with. When had their understanding of him shifted? What was the incident, the date? He thought again of the children and a shiver creased his shoulders.

"Do you notice them changing?" he asked. "The pair of them?"

"Ljuba and Dushko?" Sasho shrugged. "Maybe they're a little . . ." But his words trailed away. He couldn't find the way to describe them. They finished their coffees and still there was no word.

Minutes before the promised bus of tourists arrived, Toše skidded into Mavrovo with the announcement. Two days had passed and still no answer from Bojan, but here was something: "A bus of forty, at least!" Toše had gathered his intelligence from a friend who ran the snack stand just before the Mavrovo Park turning. "Some kind of Balkan-wide tour," said Toše: two days in Skopje followed by this stop in Mavrovo, south to Ohrid, and then into Albania and parts unknown.

"And to think they're stopping here." Sasho held one of his Skopsko-branded umbrellas as he watched for the bus. He spoke like a man preparing for a miracle, and Goran couldn't help treading in his wake. Hadn't this been what he wished years earlier, when he began arguing to build the village's touristic appeal? Only to be seen, and remembered? There was always the possibility that this group, unlike its predecessors, would perceive them in the right way, would be open to the real nature of Mavrovo, hidden for too long beneath layers of grease paint. They waited for the distant wheeze of bus brakes, and then the sleek creature itself drew into view, pulling before the hotel.

They stood alongside the bus as it released its passengers. "I like them," decided Goran. Most of the tourists wore baseball caps and long-sleeved shirts. A few had old-fashioned cameras swinging around their necks. He approached one man who stood apart from the group, and hovered a hand above his shoulder, a tentative embrace. "You aren't going to take a photo?" he asked, glancing at Toše.

Toše laughed. "Look at you!" he called. "So happy you've finally found a man you're taller than."

"A day we must never forget," said Sasho.

"Come on," said Goran, "just a quick one, on your phones." He smiled in preparation. He was at peace with these clusters of tourists, the steady thump of their roller bags tossed from the bus's belly. Was Sasho's van, the one they'd once used to drive winter skiers to the tow rope, still in good condition? "We should find the tour leader," he said, pleased that he knew this detail. "We should see if they need some entertainment for this afternoon. Maybe a hike to Gorno Selo."

Sasho scoffed. "Even I don't want to go to Gorno Selo."

"A little faster," Goran said, sensing the man moving beneath his outstretched palm. He thought of bringing this photo home to Rosa, her delight at the possibility of these new tourists who would be a little different than the old. How often did this company run their tours through Macedonia? Another question for the leader.

He was so engrossed in his visions that there was a split second when Goran didn't hear the first warbling cry, the crowd stumbling, the nervous laughter, the flash of all those cameras he'd been admiring a moment before. He still had his other version of the world. Then it broke and there was mayhem: the few tourists still straggling down from the bus were pushed by their compatriots running for the hotel, the leader using her folded red umbrella to wave them to the lobby, whose doors were flung open by a pair of tuxedoed and powdered bellboys.

"We're not going to hurt you!" Goran shouted after them. "We wouldn't hurt you! We wouldn't know how!" No one listened. They couldn't understand him, he realized as he wiped a fleck of spit from his chin. They only thought he was screaming at them, that he was angry, and maybe he was. He spun, wishing for Metchka to reveal herself behind him. There was only Sasho and Toše, laughing.

"We got your photograph," said Toše, tilting his phone's screen to Goran. And there he was, stupid grin, hand extended to a tourist whose own hands clawed before his turned face, lurching away, mouth open to a wail as if Goran—Goran who had never done a thing worse than wish his own son would stay close—might tear him to pieces.

At home, Rosa reported still no answer from Bojan. "Maybe they won't come this year," she admitted. "Maybe it's better."

Could Goran agree to this? He could not. He watched Rosa wind her apron around her hand before removing a banitsa pan of rice and chicken from the oven. Neighbors stopped by and together they sat in plastic chairs in the courtyard, sipping from the good coffee cups with flowers petaling their slender handles. "Are you listening at all?" Rosa asked at one point and Goran started, flushing and scattering cigarette ashes across his pants. The neighbors had seen the tourists climbing back in their bus not long after their arrival.

"Not leaving?" Goran asked.

"No," they said, and he slumped back into his chair. They had only gone to Bigorski Monastery and would be back in the evening.

"They won't pass it on their way to Ohrid?"

No again; the tourists would take the road north out of Mavrovo Park in the morning, so they could take the better road south.

Goran watched Metchka napping in the shade, dusty nose set between her paws. So they were only a waystation, a convenient place for this group to set their bags on their way to more interesting locales. Though he bore no responsibility for the hotel, Goran couldn't help recalling the day he'd proposed summer vacation packages, Sasho's and Toše's laughter at his scheme to stop Mavrovo's vanishment. He felt he owned everything that had come since. He dropped his cigarette and rubbed his sandaled foot over it, wishing to do the same to the day: to crush the brief and glancing desire he'd felt to render every screaming tourist and false ghost into an indecipherable nothing soon forgotten in the woodsmoked air. He didn't want to think of the camp, of how many children and families might encroach on the village when it opened, of how their collective gazes might move him a step further from the man he'd always understand himself to be.

"Have you seen Dushko and Ljuba?" he asked the group, interrupting.

"Honestly, Goran." Rosa made an apology to the guests. She invited them to stay; it was almost time to eat.

"I'm not hungry," said Goran. He stood and dusted his hands on his pants and hesitated, unable to meet Rosa's gaze. "I just need to find them," he said, holding his hands out to signal apology, no harm held here. "You stay," he told Metchka when she tried to follow.

He was unsure where the children would be. For years they had followed him around the village, setting their damp prints in the shadows of his own, waiting in the corners of rooms in their moss-draggled scarves. When had that changed? When the hotel opened? Before? Could he be in a fight with them, like the false ghosts said, and not even realize it?

Goran found himself at the lake, looking at the church. He had no memory of a time when it had been on dry land, surrounded by other aspects of the village, the homes that people had stripped of windows and roofs and furniture before the dam's flood washed over them. If he could go to the church—if he could stand on that hump of land and see Dushko and Ljuba where they spent their days—it would mean the Ghost Hotel's stories weren't true. That they had no real force.

He waited until dark, whiling away the hours at Sasho's. The bus returned and the tourists wandered the village, some carrying jars of monk-produced honey. Several pointed to him and paused for photographs, and he imagined what they must be saying. Here was the cruelest ghost of Mavrovo, enjoying a respite from his revenge, gathering caffeinated strength for another night of mayhem. Goran couldn't so much as glance at the tourists, not wanting to find the new ways he would be twisted into the figure they thought him to be. Toše sped up in his park service Jeep and laughed at Goran's glum countenance.

"The only way to deal with them," he said, "is to not think of them."

"Fine," said Goran, "but I have to go."

He tucked a few bills beneath the ashtray and walked to the

water. He imagined the hotel's activity schedule: *Seven o'clock, local ghost gets up to trouble.* Well, here he was, serving his one true purpose. He bent and removed his boots, hung his socks over the cuff. The damp pebbles shifted beneath his feet and he stood, settling himself, before stepping into the water.

Exclamations rose along the shore. Sasho's and Toše's faint laughter. Beneath the water the pebbles grew mossy and slick, and Goran held his arms outstretched as he waded to his knees. Water lapping his hips, he slipped and lost his face beneath the surface. When he opened his eyes there was nothing there, only the black-green sway of the lake.

"Look how unhappy the ghosts are," someone said when he rose. A local tour guide? Her voice, and the translating murmurs, caught on the water. "There's a reason they haven't left their village, some vengeance they're yet to take . . ."

Goran looked away from shore. He walked slower, with care, until he arrived at the church's door. When was the last time he'd been here? Easter, perhaps, though he could only remember making those midnight circles around the church rebuilt on dry land, trying not to stumble with his wavering candle. The mountain-chilled water lapped his ankles as he leaned into the door; then he was in the sanctum, the floor dry but muddled with layers of dirt and moss and fragrantly rotting plants. When he lifted the door and forced it back shut, the church held him in its quiet and black.

It bore little resemblance to his expectation. There were no pews—taken, he realized, for the new church built after the dam. The stairs to the upper level laid in a twisted heap on the silt floor. The walls, which he at first thought to be blank, revealed shadows of their former saints when his vision adjusted: water-marked men in robes, eyes scratched from their faces. So this was where Dushko had spent all his years. Goran watched the gradations of black and gray that composed the sanctum. He listened for voices. "Dushko?" he called. "Ljuba?" No answer.

He spun from wall to wall, trying to imagine this place a home. Days with no sound but the lake's faint lapping, the drip of water along the walls. Even with their eyes missing he had the sense of the saints watching him. Unnerving to feel these paintings so close, when he couldn't find any sense for the children's presence. Overhead was a faint shuffle. Damp spread between his shoulder blades. "Dushko?" he called again. He could find no grappling path to the upper level.

The moment of relief he'd felt on simply setting foot in the church—proving the story wrong!—faded in the continued silence. Would Dushko and Ljuba be here, if he were not? His wet clothes clung to him and Goran shivered, folding himself against a wall where the altar had once stood. He waited for the children to appear, for the calm of their presence as he hadn't felt it in years.

It was with a start of shame that Goran woke, spackled with light. His pants were mudpasted to his legs, and his shirt stiff. "Dushko?" he asked. "Ljuba?" Nothing. He called their names again, louder. He shouted and the only answer was his own voice. He receded into silence, pausing at the door to listen, fearing a group of tourists gathered with their flashbulbs on the other side, ready with a new story about his amplifying war against these children who had done nothing more than die and not know how to leave.

Easing through, he found the village empty and still, the lake glistening. He swam to shore but could not bring himself to place his face in the water. If he swam the other way, past the church and toward the lake's center—that was where his first home was, his and Dushko's, buried by now into the lakebed. He had never swum that far, he rarely ventured into the water at all, and he felt fortunate that the previous night it had been too dark to see anything when he found himself below the surface. What if he had opened his eyes and found a village that didn't match his dead memories?

On shore, he retrieved his boots and carried them home. Metchka barked and stood with her paws balanced on the fence. "Hello, hello," Goran said, pressing his nose to the walnut lump between her ears. Metchka who might be with him forever, if he had the luck.

Rosa stepped out in her apron, hair tied back beneath a flowered scarf. Goran was unsure how to meet her gaze. "I'll call Bojan," he said before she could speak. "I'll call him myself."

She nodded but wouldn't step aside. "Not like that," she said, pointing to his shirt, his pants.

Goran nodded. Mud pasted his hands and fell in clods as he removed the clothes, Metchka watching with cocked head.

"Don't think that dog is going inside either," said Rosa as he washed his hands. "Don't think I'm washing your clothes."

Her admonitions were a pleasure, a normalcy. Goran found his phone attached to a charging cable. Rosa had always been better at communicating, better at understanding what their son wanted for his family and why. He tried to forget his last conversation with Bojan—"You've always wanted me to be as trapped as you are," and on, and on—as he found his name in the Skype app.

The phone rang. The narrow bands of his damp undershirt chafed. Goran considered what he might say. That he needed his son to return as a balance to all the wrong views? That he needed one breathing person who saw him not as a marker of a fading place? But these would not be the right things to say, he knew. Better to say the other truths: I miss you. I want to hold my granddaughter on my lap. I want to see you. I want to see you. He moved to the window and shifted the curtain aside so he could watch Rosa in the yard, petting the dog she claimed had no hold on her. And there, crouched beneath the wavering laundry, were Dushko and Ljuba, mittens trailing from the ends of their sleeves. Before Goran could think what to make of this there was an answer, the screen showing at first only his own blank square in the corner. Then his son's voice, thick with sleep, Bojan's face clarifying as he said to hold on, just a minute, and stepped into the light.

AT NIGHT

Akshay Shrivastava

I remember when I was twelve, we lived next to this old man who would get up in the middle of the night to fix dead cars. I knew little about him except that those cars on his back lot were clearly junked, beyond any hope of repair. According to his daughter, he used to work at an auto shop before the dementia set in, and had kept the clunkers for keepsakes. Some nights I would watch him at work through my bedroom window. I saw him gather his tools from the shed and hobble out back, trip the rusted hood latches with a screwdriver, and start digging into the engines underneath for signs of life. I couldn't imagine what was going through his mind. Maybe some part of him knew he was in a fugue state, but he couldn't break out of it. I pictured him lying awake every night watching the ceiling, trapped in his head, unable to keep himself from rising up and getting back to work. After all these years, it was the only thing his body remembered how to do. Before I turned thirteen we ended up leaving that neighboring apartment, but some nights I could still hear him working the graveyard shift, the metal tools tumbling through his fingers and clattering to the ground.

We moved again when I was fifteen, and then again when I was seventeen, and then my parents changed apartments twice more after I left for college. For some reason my father could never stay in one place very long. Just when my mother and I were getting used to our current place—the layout of our rooms, the sticky cabinet doors, the neighborhood crowd—suddenly we were packing our things again and being carted off to the next. I didn't know why he felt the need to keep doing this to us. I figured it had something to do with the fact that he was never able to put together a down payment on a house. At the same time, he never seemed satisfied with any of the cramped living arrangements we found ourselves in. Coming to the States had shown him that better opportunities were always out there, and so, if a better rental deal ever surfaced, in a few months we would be getting ready to pack up and leave again. Some nights I even heard him getting a head start when he thought we were sleeping. I listened to him fumble and curse, trying to fit everything we had into boxes, and a part of me wondered if he had as little control over his decisions as my mother and I did.

Ten years after moving out, I found myself on the opposite end of the country, pulling over to the side of the road in a borrowed CR-V. I stepped out into the clear Oakland summer, slammed the door shut behind me, and leaned back against it for a better view of the property I'd bought with my own money: the first of its kind in my family's history. Pale blue paneling against pale blue sky, it held a place of relative grandeur between the two squat, white-washed duplexes on either side. It stood two stories tall and I had parked across the street to take in all of it at once. The sun was high, squinting through the branches of the tree in front of my lot. I made a visor of my hands to fend off the sun, holding every detail of it in my mind, the first Shigri-owned property in the United States, before phoning my mother and telling her what I was looking at. She started to cry. I waited, knowing what it meant to her.

We had endured twenty years of my father's luckless searching and two thousand miles of separation to arrive at this moment. After college I had decided to stay back on the West Coast instead of returning home like I'd promised. The rent was high but the salaries higher, the opportunities greater, for a fresh graduate with my standing. I lived cheaply, visited rarely, and over time saved enough to afford this place on my own. So I listened to my mother's weeping and didn't rush her to speak, or worse, hand me over to my father. Already I knew how he was going to react. *I trust you know what you're doing*, he would probably say, in a manner suggesting I didn't. What else was there for him to say? He had disowned any responsibility for my life decisions from the day I decided to stay out west. Now it was too late to lay a claim on my success, to acknowledge I had secured our family's place in this country without admitting to himself he had failed to do the same.

She was going to hand me over to him any moment. I braced myself, only to be caught off-guard when my mother's words landed harder than his. "Obaid," she said, sniffling, "that's all very good, but when are you coming home for real?" I didn't know what to say. By "home" she meant a studio apartment in East Brunswick I had only ever seen over Skype calls, that they had moved into only a few years ago, where my mother's things were probably still sitting in boxes instead of drawers, suitcases instead of closets, awaiting the next big switch, whenever it came. *This is my home now*, I wanted to tell her, but the words got stuck in my throat. I wanted to show her the house one more time, but when I looked at the picture taken on my cell phone camera, I saw in it only what she would see: a big empty building with nothing and no one inside to make it a home.

That night I lay awake on the air mattress in the master bedroom, the only article of furniture in the entire house. I turned away from the blinking eyes of the router and searched the plaster patterns on my ceiling, thinking about everything I would need to acquire in order to make my house livable. The pipes would need to be replaced, first of all, the sinks and tubs re-caulked, the yard outside tended to, and new furniture would have to be bought. My inflatable mattress would need to be switched for a bed. In time, I would need to get married and have kids, and find new jobs that paid more so I could furnish the living space with my salary increases: whatever it would take to be free of my father's doubts and my mother's tears for good. I listened as the itinerary in my head became longer and longer, and even when I tried to fall asleep, I couldn't shut out the noise. It was the rattle in my father's brain, the one that shook him awake in the dead of night and urged him to fill empty boxes that would never find their destination. It was the sound of the old man next door tinkering with dead engines. I heard his tools falling to the floor. With trembling hands he would retrieve them and get back to work, fixing those things that no one had ever asked or needed him to fix in the first place.

QUESTION FOR MY BROTHER
RE: WARP DRIVE, THE SPEED OF LIGHT

Emily Cinquemani

Imagine an ant, you say
    as we eat sandwiches
at the table, windows already December
    dark. Imagine it at the end
of this placemat, the way it
    would look out over warp
and weft and see an eternity—

    its insect brain unable
to untangle each ridge of weave
    or envision an end. You
brush crumbs off the brown fabric
    square, which is now
space-time, and fold it so its edges
    touch. We watch

the invisible ant step from end
    to end. Then you let go,
and the cloth sprawls open.
    Younger sibling of physics
and logic, of the universe mapped
    out in ten dimensions,
you say that this is how we might
    move faster than light, say
did you know black holes
    would sound like static
between radio stations if we
    could hear them? You

explain that scientists saw matter
    squared and knew it could be
negative, anti, ready to annihilate,
    its other. Is there easy

math for the world—
    casually violent, reeling
up on the TV in the coffee shop,
    scrolled over, regular
enough to warrant the usual how
    did we let this happen? Alone
in my new city, I often feel far
    away from everything,
a soft pang stuck somewhere
    in the back of my throat
like the throb of prodding burnt
    skin with my tongue. Tell me
again that darkness hums

    static while it drinks fistfuls
of light. Say there's evidence
    that we might pass over
fields of life woven too wide
    to cross. And, when we can't
move, who is it that bends
    to fold up the space beneath us?

THE MYSTIC MARRIAGE
OF SAINT CATHERINE OF SIENA

Molly Guinn Bradley

It's a shock when David Sampson says that Salome is the most beautiful girl in our class. Of course she is, by far, with long, thick hair the color of honey wheat, a tiny face with vulpine features, slim, wide-set eyes, and enchanted skin. But it seemed as though no one else—none of the boys, that is—had noticed. She's so quiet it's easy to miss her. But we see her. We know.

Sampson is the class stoner and should be the class clown, but he's usually too stoned to finish his sentences. He was, until senior year, a large, soft boy, almost cuddly, if he hadn't reeked of weed and stale cigarettes. He wore the same oversized navy hoodie every day, covering his close-shaved head like a robe, and he spoke in a drone so soft he might have been praying. But if you listened, he usually wasn't saying anything good. He liked dirty jokes, dead baby jokes. He told sexist jokes, too, but since we shot him dirty looks, we mostly assumed he was telling them just to get a rise out of us. Besides, the ones he told were the kind with no teeth. His favorite was a silly inversion of a clichéd directive: *Get in the sandwich and make me a kitchen.* We have to admit, the first time we heard it, we laughed.

His mom is a feminist historian who came to our social studies class to give a talk one day. We'd never seen Sampson slump so low in his chair or pull his hoodie so far down over his face so that only his angular chin showed. His mom gave him a hard time that day, asking him questions that, shockingly, he knew the answers to. "'I will everywhere make humanity more than sex.' Words spoken by . . . David, can you tell us?" His mother extended a long, manicured finger in her son's direction. A long pause, and then from beneath the hoodie came a mumble. "That's right: Lucy Blackwell. Now, in the 1850s . . ." We all felt kind of bad for Sampson that day. He made more sense to us after that. He became softer in our eyes. He didn't seem to mind.

In the fall of our senior year, we come back to find Sampson transformed. He's dropped probably forty pounds. He wears the same oversized sweatshirt that truly is a robe now, draping off his frame, and his face is gaunt. He has let his hair grow, and the curls on his head are a shock of gold. He looks older and harder, but delicate, almost beautiful.

Then we learn (we don't remember who told us first) he's been sleeping with Salome all summer. At first none of us really believes it. The pairing seems inconceivable. Besides, so few of the rest of us have had sex—we who are more solid and vibrant and interesting than Salome; we who, even if we aren't exactly gorgeous or cool or beloved, at least have a presence, a reputation, skills that we put on display in English and choir and theater, teachers who like us more than the others, we who go to nerdy summer programs in college dorms that make us seem sophisticated each time we come back in the fall.

Salome is one of the quiet girls, would be indistinguishable from the rest if it weren't for her beauty. We see her set her notebook and pencil case (she still carries a pencil case) neatly on her desk in French class; we see her put her hand up in Trig. We watch her chew salad with her mouth closed at lunchtime and staple her English papers parallel to the top edge. We are aware of her the way you're aware of the mechanics behind every clock and inside every wristwatch: astonishing when you look at it, but you don't often look. But it's nice to know she's there.

Anyway, it's just not fair. Not that we want to have sex with Sampson. That would be absurd. But we want, at least, to be desired, to be found beautiful—to be discovered. We want someone unusual to push past all the powdered and curled and well-dressed girls in our grade, drawn by our own unusual magnetism, and find us.

But we're also afraid of exactly this. For as unusual as we secretly hope we are, we're also terrified that someone will discover we are not. Better to remain a compelling mystery than become a corporeal disappointment.

In a move that none of us expect, Sampson turns up to audition for the high school play. The play is a big deal for those of us who have elected to take theater every semester and showed up religiously for every single rehearsal for every single production.

Sampson walks in like it only occurred to him to come five minutes before auditions began.

And we are even more surprised to find that he is, somehow, good. At first, we can't tell if maybe we're just thrown by the body he inhabits that we barely recognize. Its movements are quicker, its gestures finer, its angles sharper. It becomes apparent that in this new body he is inventing movement, is creating its own idiosyncratic language before our very eyes. He is a new animal, a species we can't identify.

When the casting sheet is posted on the bulletin board outside the auditorium, we are not surprised to learn that he has landed the lead. With Sampson at the helm, the usual dynamic shifts; the game has changed. An outsider has joined us, and we get to show him our world.

In French class, Salome has taken to sitting in the back corner. We don't notice until Madame calls her out. *"Tu es moins sérieuse cette année, Salomé?"* she says, too confident in the response she'll receive. To everyone's surprise, though Salome squeezes out a small smile for Madame, the instant after she turns back to the whiteboard Salome rolls her eyes. We are stunned and impressed. We are just a little bit jealous. Before, when she made herself small and quiet, Salome's power lay dormant. Now she holds it in her hands, admiring its every facet, and it glows.

In rehearsals, Sampson is his usual goofy self, but when he gets to work he is utterly sober. This is the first time we've seen him go quiet immediately when a teacher speaks to him. It's partly the hypnotic power of our director, whose elvish qualities and spritely energy are impossible not to fall in love with. We watch her give him direction and see him really listen, spinning her instructions in his head, making something private that we can't see. It's the first time it really occurs to us that Sampson has a secret self, just like the rest of us—one where he gets to be the person we have not yet let him be. But something is reeling him out, little by little. Or maybe we are actually, finally seeing him for the first time.

Salome's friends were two mousy girls with interchangeably forgettable names. One of them liked to tell anyone who'd listen about her aspirations to become a dermatologist, because of how much she loved securing a pimple between her two fingernails and slowly applying pressure until the pus burst. The other seemed to become nervous beyond reason whenever we spoke to her, so we generally didn't.

But we don't see Salome with these girls anymore. We see them sitting together at lunch, business as usual, but Salome isn't there. We don't know where she goes. We don't see Sampson, either, but we've never known where he goes when he's not around. We've never particularly cared, until now. Now we find ourselves not only aware of his movements, of his orbit around school, but curious about them.

One day, leaving school, we see him and Salome across the street at the gas station. He's leaning against a car—her family's—and her reedy body leans against his, standing between his legs. It strikes us how beautiful they both are. It's almost striking enough to keep us from feeling the jolt of something like betrayal. But that's silly. We are only borrowing him. Someone else got to him first.

Sampson still makes jokes that make us cringe. But at Saturday rehearsals, he makes sure there is enough pizza for everyone when we break for lunch. He lets us know when there are crumbs in our hair. He teases us, but he never pushes too hard. He recognizes that some of us are more delicate than we used to be. He is more delicate than he used to be.

When we ride the late bus home from play practice, Sampson is one of us, joking and laughing about all the same things. But in the morning, on the regular bus to school, Sampson either talks to his non-play friends or is quiet. He doesn't talk to us.

Late one night at a long rehearsal, we sit with Sampson at the side of the stage during a break. He has taken to wandering over to us between scenes, striking up mundane conversations that we wouldn't have the energy for if it were anyone else. The mundanity of conversations with him is imbued with something that makes us smile and smirk and fidget. We want to hear every dull syllable that comes from his lips.

"We should get food," he says.

We laugh. We tell him we're surprised: it doesn't look like he eats much these days. We're trying to tease him, or maybe compliment him, but our concern slides out headfirst.

"I was too fat," he says. "Now I'm too skinny. That's why we should get food. I'm going to waste away."

Then he looks at me and says, "You've gotten skinny, too." He takes my hand, its back facing up, and tells me to lift my fingers up by the knuckles. "See?" He taps each one of the long, delicate bones that protrude in response. "You don't have any meat on you."

"Neither do you," I say.

We look at each other. Our director calls us to attention. But I can hear his mind still purring next to mine, like he and I are by ourselves in an adjoining room.

At the end of rehearsal, Sampson asks me where I live. "I ride your bus," I say. "Every day."

"No way," he says. "How didn't I know this? Why didn't you tell me?" He faces me. "We should go get food. Let's get food sometime."

"Okay," I say. "Let's." And I know that we won't, but I'm praying we do.

We talk about it, how Sampson wants to get food with me. One of us says, "He has such a huge crush on you, Catherine. He gets so flustered when he's around you."

"I don't think so," I say, with a laugh. "He has Salome."

"I mean, yeah, they're fucking, but he *likes* you."

"It's like, he wants her, but he *adores* you."

I don't understand the difference, but we laugh it off. It's sweet that he likes me, that he's trying so hard. It's funny, to think about getting food with Sampson. We can hardly imagine it!

But Sampson doesn't mention getting food again for a long time. We assume that he was joking, or was stoned and forgot about it, or maybe he changed his mind. Maybe he was just hungry.

In French class, we match verbs with appropriate objects. The verbs are *acheter, aimer, oublier, adorer, saluer*—to buy, to love, to forget, to adore, to greet. The objects are *abricots, devoirs, amis, cahiers, Dieu*—apricots, homework, friends, notebooks, God.

We go around the room. "*J'achète les amis,*" says a boy in the back, snickering before he's even finished his sentence. We would be amused, but it's like this every day, and we are tired. He looks to Salome for approval, who does not look at him. She seems tired, too.

When it's my turn, I say, "*J'adore les abricots.*"

"*Non, non,*" says our French teacher. "*On* aime *les abricots. On adore* Dieu."

We're in class when we hear commotion in the hallway. The door to our classroom is open. One of the English teachers is walking briskly down the hall, trailed by a lanky, smirking Salome. Our teacher pauses slightly to watch, but the trouble falls from his face just as quickly as it landed, and we resume.

When class lets out, we walk to the cafeteria for lunch and hear whispers that Salome, noticeably addled in class, was suspended for being stoned at school. As we're digesting this, we see Sampson cut through the crowd in the hall, his bag dangling from one shoulder. The head of upper school is close behind. "Mr. Sampson," he calls, "please don't let this turn out poorly for you, too." But he's already gone, the door swinging apologetically behind him.

We're stunned. Some of us are impressed. Some of us feel like Salome has gone too far. We frame it in worry—we're concerned for what's happening to her; we wonder if everything is okay—but we're not worried. Secretly, we're a little relieved. The awe we've felt for her has been tempered by consequence. No one's burden is that light.

Performances begin. We're nervous and excited and our energy spills off the stage, literally: in the first performance, someone accidentally knocks a plate into the orchestra pit, where it shatters to the sound of laughter and applause. Fortunately there was no orchestra in the pit, or things might have ended differently.

As the shows go on, we watch each other, really watch each other. We've all grown so much since we each slipped timidly into our roles like a chrysalis at the start of rehearsals. Now we are magnificent. We speak our lines like they're our own words, as easy as thinking, as easy as hope. We will miss the intimacy our characters share when this ends. We will miss the close physical space the play has forced our bodies to inhabit together.

We're thinking about this onstage and off, in the wings while we're waiting for our cue. We're thinking about it just before our final entrance, while we stand alone in the wings. Then there is another presence, a breath, beside me like a ghost, but this is a ghost I know. Two slender hands alight on my waist, and when I don't move away, they encircle me, and the body that belongs to them nests itself behind me. I have never been touched this way. I can feel every curve of his body even though he barely hovers behind me, his touch so light. I feel so light. I thread my fingers through his and I feel, for the first time in a year, more than the thrill of the stage or the draw of Salome's beauty or the divinity of an empty stomach. This is adoration.

He and I stand there in the dark, our sad, hard edges locked together to make something larger than ourselves, until we hear our cue. And so he and I break apart, and he and I drift onstage, and we resume our roles.

The play ends. Things go back to normal. We go back to riding the four o'clock bus home. We're relieved, but a little sad. It feels like a larger kind of ending.

The season changes, and so does the light. It streams long and late through our classroom windows onto our desks. It shoots and bends through the bus like a prism. We are illuminated. We feel, however fleetingly, like we're coming alive.

Here at the end of the year, all of us about to go our separate ways, everyone changes. It's sort of sudden, but when it happens it's like we knew it would happen all along. It's like the curtain has fallen at the end of the play that has been our time at this school, and we're leaving the theater, freed from the characters we have played for so long. We are finally ourselves.

People talk to us who have never really talked to us before. People do things they've never done before. Some of us get wasted at the graduation party and find ourselves embracing people we thought we hated. Some of us are a little drunk, leaning against a wall at the graduation party, watching our friends, when Salome appears.

"Come to the balcony," she says. Then she takes my hand, and we thread through the throng of all kinds of people I suddenly don't care about as she leads me there.

Waiting on the balcony is Sampson. He smiles, then exchanges a look with Salome.

"So," Salome says, "we heard you wanted to try this."

I stare. Then Sampson produces what looks like a skinny, hand-rolled cigarette.

"Oh," I say, "it's really okay." But Salome has already taken it and lit it, and she puts it to her perfect lips, inhales deeply. Then she passes it to Sampson, who takes a drag, and then offers it to me. Hesitantly I take it, lift it to my lips as they watch.

"I don't know how to do this," I admit.

"Just breathe," says Salome. I expect her to be impatient with me, but she's smiling, eager, like we're all in on something together.

I inhale and then cough. Sampson pats me on the back, and when I can finally take a breath, I see they're looking at me expectantly. I'm about to give them a smile, to signal I'm okay, when it comes over me: the lightness I've been chasing all year, that I've only found onstage or in an empty stomach, or just one other time, when Sampson held me in the dark.

We pass the joint around as the sun sets behind the city skyline, until I can't take anymore. Salome and Sampson talk a little, but I'm content to just listen to the sound: the music of two voices that know each other so well they've become seamless.

"I'm going to miss you guys," says Salome. For an instant in her voice I hear the old Salome, the shy, quiet one—the one I thought everyone had missed but me. Then I think: Maybe there is no old Salome. Maybe she never really changed. Maybe it's us who started seeing her differently. Then I remember we're all high.

"You won't miss me that much," I say with a laugh. "We didn't really hang out."

"I always thought we might," she says. "Anyway, it's been nice to know you're there."

We're quiet again. "You feel okay?" Sampson says to me.

I nod, but in the dark he can't see the motion. The lightness rolls in waves. I take a breath and reach my hand out, and as I do I feel his reaching out toward mine.

POST-ROMANTIC
Melissa Studdard

Name your baby after the sexless
night in the Jacuzzi

because there are at least
five different ways to arrive

at nothing. Five different ways
to interpret a butterfly

stoned by the river.
A night of passion stoned

by an overcast soul. Even
if you're committed

to bringing your own
foreplay, you may find

that the catalogue
of your mistakes

is greater than
the charm of your ass.

But, love?
That's another story.

Told by fools
and prophets.

Carved into wind.

LAST DANCE
IN A MEADOWLAND OF THE FLESHLESS

Jeremy Halinen

All his teeth:
perfect,

                        unchipped,
                        readily
            apparent
            due

to his lack
of lips.

                        One over each
                        of my trapezii

                  I dangled
                  his humeri

after first
cuffing

                      his carpals
                      so he

       couldn't
         let go,
rested
his skull in

                      the nest
                      of my shoulder,
              and with
              my left arm

bracing his
rib cage

                      whispered,
                      Follow

         my lead.
         I placed

my right hand
where his

           heart
           had been
     but felt
     only rib-
split wind.
As hip to hipbone

           fro and to
           we swayed

    lentissimo,
     gusts
perhaps
his spirits

           rattled
           his phalanges
     and tapped
     my back
with them
like gentlemen

           eager
           to cut in.

YES, BUT IT'S A TINY FIRE
Robert Wood Lynn

The whole state of California's burning. Mom saw it on the news. Quails. Cactuses. Palm trees. Everything going up. "Call your little brother," she tells me on the phone, though I don't see how that's supposed to help. If David is on fire, talking could only slow him down. And if he's not on fire, what do we have to talk about?

Mom asks if I've seen *Genome PI* yet. I get all pissed off and don't know why. Two detectives solve crimes with a DNA swab and a family tree. Good TV, I guess. Mom asks what I'd do if David was accused of a crime and the cops needed my saliva to prove it. Would I cooperate? Jesus. I realize it's her *yet* that's making me mad, its implication of inevitability. The assumption that I'm sitting there on Tuesday nights watching the news and then whatever comes on after the news and then whatever comes on after that, which is *Genome PI*. Mom starts recounting an episode where they catch the Golden State Killer. She tells me Golden State means California and I need to hang up. I am sick of hearing about that place and even more sick of being told I don't know anything about it.

When I imagine California, I imagine it not like the movies. More like a fuse burning in a cartoon, running down the spine of the West Coast, waiting to blow. I picture the whole thing in flames and David just sitting there as Santa Rosa burns around him. I try not to imagine California.

"I have to go call David," I tell Mom. But then I don't. David doesn't mind. He never calls me either.

It's a reasonable seventy-six degrees here in Waynesboro, Virginia and nothing is on fire. Mom's in her new boyfriend's house in Staunton and nothing's on fire there either. I have court in the morning, though I'm trying not to think about it.

Around six I drive down to BG's apartment on the other side of the river in Basic City. Basic's a real piece of shit and BG's place is no different. It's a basement-level apartment in a long, triangular building that takes the shape of its lot. Most of the thing is hallway. At least it's his. Not to say I mind having Mom's house to myself—lord knows I couldn't swing rent on my own. The house just doesn't count as mine since I'm not allowed to mess with the decor. All her glass cabinets full of antique dolls, those nautical stars on the wall.

BG's apartment, on the other hand, is him all the way. Spare and unsentimental. Industrial carpeting and a TV stand and couch. On the end table—the only table—there's a framed picture of the two of us from high school. It's just about the only decoration in his place that isn't a football jersey. I used to think this was sweet until I realized I gave it to him when we graduated seven years ago. It reigns over the apartment by default. I worry that's how I function in his life.

The only place to sit is the couch, which I like for its intimacy. On days we get drunk here, I like to lay my legs across his even though—or maybe because—I know it makes him uncomfortable. Today we're both sober as judges.

I ask him what he's wearing to court in the morning.

"Gameday decision," he says, everything a sports metaphor.

I tell him to show me and he protests a bit but not hard. BG will do what I ask, long as it's small. Where to eat, what to watch. Never the big stuff, like letting me hold a hundred bucks or moving out of state.

He comes out of his bedroom in a checked shirt, a little wrinkly but tucked in. His tie, untied, hangs all the way down to his balls, makes him look like some sort of off-brand pastor.

"Got a suit that goes with it, but tonight I can't be bothered."

He looks cute, honestly. Not confident. BG has a way of taking up all the space in a room when you can tell he wants to take up none. Especially a room this small. I catcall him as he walks the runway of his narrow living room. "Lookin' fine baby. Yougottaboyfriend? You want one?" I know BG likes the attention even if he doesn't show it. I catch a half smile as he goes to change back into a hoodie.

While he does, I stand outside the closed door to his bedroom, where he's got an old Garfield page-a-day calendar comic taped to it. Garfield's in his bed and John asks him if he's gonna get up and Garfield says he doesn't feel like it, and then John says, *Your blanket's on fire.* And Garfield, still tucked in, says, *Yes, but it's a tiny fire.* I remember giving it to BG at school one day in eighth grade—April 7, 2006, I guess—but I didn't expect him to keep it forever. Once, it made me laugh, and now it's an epitaph for how much it used to make me laugh.

BG's real name is Brandon Gluck, but he's never gone by anything other than BG. He doesn't have a middle name. Back in school, everybody called him BG Gluck. When people asked what the G stood for, he said Gluck. And they'd say, "Yeah, but the other G?" And BG would say, "What other G?"

This caught on, and people started doing it for shits. Just to see him fume. They'd goad newcomers into asking, which is around when BG took to punching anyone who asked in the mouth. To avoid this, we took to calling him Double Gluck but eventually that got shortened to Double G, which didn't solve the problem at all.

BG and his brother Lyle lost their college funds when their mom went all in on Beanie Babies right before the bubble burst in December of '99. Everybody knew it too, since for years after she'd park on the side of Route 250 right off the interstate and spread those little plush bears out on the roof of her car trying to sell them at pre-crash prices. Just standing there chain-smoking and screaming at anyone she thought was driving too fast. Everybody drives too fast here.

BG got teased about Beanie Babies a lot and if you tease BG he's liable to punch you in the mouth. We met in detention.

At thirteen, he was twice my size and talked at half my speed. He had a small voice you'd never guess came from such a big dude. He liked thumb wrestling because he was the best at it and he was the best at it because he had the biggest, softest hands and to say I fell in love with him the first time I touched them wouldn't be all that far off.

David texts a picture to the family group thread of himself in a swimming pool, the in-ground kind. Haze all around. He adds, "we're safe here no matter what." There's an inflatable pizza floatie in the background but no sign of who the *we* is. Gramma responds with the hearts-for-eyes emoji. If I go to jail tomorrow I'm not telling these assholes a thing.

We go to the Luncheonette for dinner because it's almost cheaper than cooking and right down the street. We don't even have to drive. BG orders a hotdog and a side of grits and I get a grilled cheese and a Coke. I'm trying to switch to Diet but I still wince at the taste every time. Halfway through the meal, a line cook comes out of the kitchen with a plate of fried green tomatoes and a spatula, asking folks if they'd like any. He doles some out on our plates, free.

BG smiles big. "Tell you what, they don't have this in California."

"You don't know that," I say. But he's probably right. David says California's full of avocado hamburgers for sixteen dollars a pop.

The waitress comes back to ask if everything's good. She's about our age, maybe twenty-five. Skinny with a sharp face. Looks like someone we went to school with but so does everybody.

"Yup," BG says to her. "My boy here wants to move outta town but the food's gonna make him stay." She's new here, they always are—no one makes a career out of the Luncheonette. BG talks like he knows her, which puts me off.

"Where you looking to go?" she asks me.

"California," I say. "Or New York. Somewhere they—"

"Can you believe that?" BG jumps in. "He wants to go from Waynesboro, the very place where Spandex was invented, to some city where all people do is buy it?"

She laughs and I hate that she does. Does he come here without me?

"What're you mad about?" BG says to me when she leaves.

"I'm not mad."

"I can tell cause you're clenching your jaw off-center."

"No," I say, centering it back. "It's just, if you're gonna flirt, you could at least leave me out of it." When it comes to BG and women, I can't actually tell the difference between flirting and talking but it makes me angry either way.

"Sorry," he says, always quick to apologize for the shit he shouldn't have to. Never the rest.

We try not to talk about tomorrow but that makes it hard to talk at all.

"It's just a misdemeanor," I say after a while.

"You ever been arrested before?"

"No." I'm ashamed of the answer, though there's no reason I should be. I know BG hasn't either. We don't get into any shit, but as Mom says, everything runs out eventually and luck ain't different.

"Shonna's brother said even if they put us in jail, County's not all that bad. He usually gets his set up as work release, weekends only."

It's not that jail scares me, though it does. But a conviction means I can't teach, here or anyplace probably. That I've wasted all this work toward my degree.

BG continues. "He said whatever the judge gives you gets halved by the system. So a thirty-day sentence is really just fifteen served. Even less since you don't do a full day on either end for intake and release."

I've stopped listening. I want to tell BG that I'm afraid. He doesn't look it so I don't.

I suggest we go up to the fire tower on Elliot's Knob and get high. "You know, since the weather's nice." The way we used to all the time. Haven't in a minute. I don't have any weed though, so I'd be mooching off his.

BG says he promised his brother he'd go to bed early and make a good showing for the judge.

"Who from your family is coming?" he asks me, but I get up to pay the check instead of answering. Twelve dollars for the both of us. It makes me angry sometimes, living here. That there's no place cheaper to go. No softer place to land.

"The only safe place to run in a wildfire is to ground that's already been burned. That's what David says," Mom tells me when I call her on the way home. He's not evacuating yet, might not. She asks about my conversation with him and I change the subject. She tells me he's got a new girlfriend. This one also works at the winery. I was gonna ask Mom to come to court in the morning, for the good showing at trial, like BG's brother told me to. But it's probably too late, she'd have to call in sick from work. And I don't want to put myself up against David's good news.

She asks me how the kids are this year. "I don't get to know them," I say, which is true, even if it omits that I got kicked off the substitute teacher list.

"Watch for deer and text when you get home," she says before we hang up. As always, I say I will and then I don't.

Fucking BG. All his fault we got caught up in that fight—it was his coworker Travis we ran into at the 7-Eleven before the high school game. We got to talking by the Slurpee machine, how BG and I were there to see my little cousin Randy kick. Trav was there to see his cousin Randy, and it turned out to be the same cousin Randy just on different sides and maybe once or twice removed—I don't keep up with how the numbers work. BG and me, we were splitting a tall boy of something high gravity to spike our Slurpees and Trav asked for some. I said no and he said, "We're family," and I said, "I sure as hell hope not," and BG ended up buying him one anyway because BG hates conflict, which is how we ended up stuck with Travis all night. Stuck walking with Travis the whole long way from the store to the game, where he talked our ears off about his sister's ex-boyfriend. Stuck hanging with Travis under the bleachers when he spotted the guy in the crowd. Stuck holding Travis back when the dude smiled at him on the way back from taking a piss—it all went to shit from there. I've always known BG was going to ruin my life but I didn't think it'd be from being a pushover about twenty-four ounces of malt liquor.

Mom's house is still empty when I get home. Haven't seen her in a few weeks now, which means it's on me to take care of the plants and the cat. I've never been any good at keeping things alive, but I water the ferns and leave some for the cat, feed it too. I like tending to my charges. Mostly I like that the word tend sounds like tender. BG called me tender once three years ago and I still think about it. I swear to god sometimes it's the only reason I still let him be my friend.

I can't sleep for shit. Jacking off usually helps, but I'm so nervous I can't stay hard. Who will keep the plants alive if I get sent up? Who feeds the cat? I resent how it's on me to arrange that, to let somebody know what's going down before anything that needs me dies. The thing about asking for help is you have to see the way someone sees you in their answer.

Around five in the morning I text David "i'm in trouble," thinking he might be awake. I can never remember the time difference, which hours jump where. First thing people do when they move away is expect you to know where they are all the time. I refuse. An act of resistance.

I see the typing dots in the text window, so I know he's seen it. I wait for his response before explaining anything, but he doesn't send one. The last text in the window is from three weeks ago, him asking when Gramma's birthday is. I never answered and it passed. I wonder if he remembered to call her. I didn't, but then again, I see her every week, which should count for something, though I know it doesn't.

In the two years David has been in California, he's been back to visit Gramma exactly once. Still, every week she has me load up YouTube, show her the clip of him on *Entertainment Tonight*. The one where he's giving a wine tasting to the cast of *Hamilton*. He's mostly in the B-roll. There's one point where he speaks, asks if they'd like to try the chardonnay. For Christmas, David got Gramma an autographed copy of the original cast recording and now she has it memorized.

I google the time in California. Shit. It's 2 a.m. there. Now I'm mad at myself for texting David. For thinking he could help, which he couldn't, even if he knew what was up. For hanging one more ornament on his tree of my fuckedupedness. But mostly I'm mad at myself for giving David a perfectly good excuse not to respond. "nvm don't tell mom," I add. I turn over to sleep but sleep doesn't come. When it finally does, I don't notice.

Waynesboro General District Court shares its parking lot with the Kroger across the way. At eight in the morning, I meet BG and his dumbass brother there, Lyle. I've never liked Lyle but he's fresh out of law school and said he'd be our lawyer for free. On his advice, we're here in our best clothes. "You cherubs don't look guilty," he says when he sees us. I'm in a light blue polo shirt and the only pair of pants I have that aren't jeans. They don't zip up all the way anymore but with a belt you can't tell.

It's really something to see BG in a suit—I've never seen him so dressed up, all these years. Not even for his mom's funeral. His tie all tied, dangling from his neck, looks sort of like a leash. With his mussed-up hair, he has the air of a dog that made a break for freedom, only to get caught in some neighbor's garden and dragged back in shame. He's beautiful.

At this hour you can't tell who's there for court and who's grabbing groceries before work. Lyle says the only other people in suits are attorneys. Unlike BG's, his is well-fitted. It's also double-breasted and tan. A stupid look, even I know that.

Lyle takes another glance at my polo shirt and tells me it's weird to show up dressed like the victim. I forgot that the kid Trav beat up was some preppy lacrosse coach from Crozet, the rich side of the mountain. I go back to my truck and scrounge around until I find a button-down in the cab, one that's been on my dashboard since spring semester, wrinkled and bleached by the sun.

At the metal detectors the bailiff tells me I can't bring my phone in the courtroom so I gotta carry it all the way back out to the truck. I check one more time to see if David has responded to my text but of course not. Is this the last time I use my phone until jail? I don't know the playbook for this. I text Mom, "I love you." I've never done that before and immediately regret how much it'll freak her out. She texts back right away, asks if I'm okay, then calls my phone before I have a chance to respond. I don't have time for this. I picture BG waiting for me at the metal detectors like a dog outside a store. Like some kid on Christmas morning expecting his dad to come back from the 7-Eleven. I feel like crying but I'm not a baby. I get it together.

"Hey Momma, I can't talk long," I say when I pick up.

"Oh, glad you're all right," she says, which is funny because I haven't said I am. Honestly, I'm not. I'm close to saying so.

"I already have David and the fires to worry about," she adds.

"Yeah totally." I guess not that close. "How's he handling them?"

"He says he's fine as long as the wind doesn't change direction."

I ask how likely that is, a genuine question. She doesn't answer. Would I bet my life on the winds not changing?

"Did you know Lauren is famous?" She talks about Lauren as if I should know who she is. "David says she was on an episode of *Say Yes to the Dress*. She said yes to the dress but never did get married. Isn't that good?"

"Isn't what good?"

"That she's not divorced. I wouldn't want David to have to deal with dating a divorcée. I bet you need a lawyer for that."

"Why would you need—" I look back at the courthouse, notice the stream of people going inside has slowed to a trickle. Without his phone, BG can't even call me to ask what's taking me so long. "Okay Mom I gotta go." I don't have a good excuse. I tell her I have a meeting but she knows I never have meetings.

"Oh, that's exciting? Something important? Like a job interview?"

"It's with a lawyer actually. I'm seeing a divorcé."

Mom laughs a little too hard for someone who's never asked me about the men I'm dating.

"Good luck with the job interview," she says.

I don't remember all that much about the fight, except we were all drunk and in a bad mood from the start—the kind Mom says comes from being young in the Shenandoah Valley. Didn't help that the game was already in the toilet. Robert E. Lee beating the shit out of Waynesboro High 28 to 12. Would've stung bad enough on its own without the rivalry game and Randy missing both extra points.

That last bit was a wreck I saw coming in slow motion. Let me tell you, as a former scrawny kid with a big leg, if a football coach comes sniffing around cross-country practice saying quit the team to come kick for the varsity, you better be damn sure you hold up under pressure. If you're like me, you joined the cross-country team cause you've got more flight than fight in you. And Randy was like me, which also meant he didn't listen for shit which also meant he embarrassed himself in front of fifteen hundred people on a Friday night. Somehow, this meant that when Travis's sister's ex-boyfriend gave us a smile, Travis tried to put the poor guy's teeth down his throat and just about succeeded.

By the time Travis was through with Austin—I didn't know the victim's name until I read the subpoena: Austin Chase Critcher, twenty-eight, of Crozet, Virginia—by the time Travis got finished with him, he was leaking red-brown from his nose and mouth like a barnyard faucet and I swear to god Travis was trying to bite the damn gator off his polo. Took three people to pry Trav off.

The whole time, BG and I just sat there sipping our Slurpees. Not that we did anything to stop it, once Trav got going, but we weren't a part of it neither. When the WPD got there, the gawkers that gathered kept referring to us with collective nouns. *That bunch. Their lot.* The cops grabbed Trav first and then after a while they went ahead and arrested BG and me too. They pressed gang charges against us, assault by mob, Virginia § 18.2-42, which says if three or more people get together to fight somebody, they're all guilty for whatever one of them does. Lyle said it's a bullshit statute, should be against the Constitution but ain't. Just like that BG lost his job at county maintenance and I got booted off the substitute teacher list pending the trial and Lyle had his first two clients from anything other than the court-appointed list.

I still don't know what Austin did to Travis's sister, but Trav's rage was unholy enough that I'd bet the guy earned it. Or maybe nobody deserves this sort of thing. I had to take a Gender in Literature class once at Blue Ridge Community College—that wheat stalk of a professor there talked all about toxic masculinity. He'd probably call what Travis did a prime case of it. Thing is, you gotta be careful not to stick that label on everything it fits on in this town. The football coach? Toxic masculinity. Randy? Toxic masculinity. The cops? Toxic. The judge? Toxic. Me and all my explosive resentment? Toxic. The way BG gets all nervous when I lean in close enough I can feel the heat of his breath? How he corrects me when I joke he's my boyfriend? Toxic as whatever

DuPont used to pump into the Shenandoah River.

Through the metal detectors, BG is waiting by himself at the edge of the mass of people. They're still not letting us in the courtroom and I feel dumb for hanging up so quick on Mom.

"Where's our goddamn lawyer?" I ask, all patience evaporated.

"He went upstairs to the clerk's office to get coffee and hit on the old ladies. His words."

"Did you tell him how I like my coffee?"

"He didn't offer to get us none," BG says.

"You didn't ask?" I snap back and I can see it shake through him like a reprimand.

"I didn't think it was allowed."

BG didn't think. Of course not. For some reason, that sets me off. Here in this overlit limbo between the metal detectors and the courtroom door, on these institutional tiles that have never been mopped, I am angry with him. For getting me into this mess. For letting me use his dumbass of a brother as a lawyer. For letting his dumbass brother get coffee for himself but not us. For never once rocking the boat. For keeping me from moving to California when he knows I want to. For letting me follow him around for a decade like a puppy, never knowing if he loved or just tolerated me. For making me the one that always calls him, that shows up at his place on Sunday afternoons and pays the bill at the Luncheonette. I think about how afraid I am of the courtroom and what could happen inside it and I look up at BG who looks back at me and mouths *I'm scared*, as if he can sense what I'm thinking.

And just like that I am crying though I know I'm not supposed to. Not here, not now, not never. I wonder what I'd do if they drag us apart in the courtroom and take us away in handcuffs, will I be allowed to hug him or tell him I love him, a fact which he already knows? Will he say it back, in his own, straight-boy way? I remind myself that this is only a goddamned misdemeanor and I'm being dramatic which only makes me feel worse. I remember that nobody is gonna die but also how much I want to. How embarrassing it is to want to. How embarrassing it is to want anything at all. To want to hold BG's biggest, softest hands. And then there is a creak and the courtroom doors open and the bailiff barks instructions and there's a rush of people, nervously charging the empty space. And most of us will go home today, but some of us will not.

For all the tough talk, I have never been inside a courtroom before. Neither has BG. We follow Lyle but he turns and stops us before we pass the bar, the swinging gate into the main chamber. "This part's lawyers only until your case is called." What makes Lyle feel good about lording it over us? We're just a couple of fuckups, criminals maybe if today goes wrong.

BG and I sit on the way-back bench. It's long, wooden, and uncomfortable, what gets called a pew in church. Funny how things get a different name in these places, even though it's the same game of dress-up and power. I've pulled myself together again. I start picking at my cuticles and look around the room ranking people in order of fuckability.

Lyle comes by after about an hour of tedious cases. Court's not like I expected. You can't hear the judge or the testimony. Everyone speaks too quiet to pick up the gory details, so all we get is the faces. Sad, angry, bored. Victims and defendants indistinguishable. Every so often the bailiff leads someone away in handcuffs, or brings people in that way, then uncuffs them to let them face the judge hands-free—though still in their gray jumpsuits with their feet all chained together.

I didn't eat breakfast and my stomach is eating itself. Lyle points out the Assistant Commonwealth's Attorney, a middle-aged woman with a perm and thick, small glasses and I watch her zip about the room with an accordion file and an iced latte, making inaudible deals or shrugging at defense attorneys. Lyle gets up to flag her down and we watch, but only watch, as they chat. If I'd eaten anything I would've thrown it up by now.

Lyle comes back from talking to the prosecutor. "Good news guys. I got you out of it."

I'm already in for the hug when BG stops me. "How?" he asks Lyle.

"You just have to plead guilty."

"That's your idea of getting out of it?" I ask. I look at BG and BG looks at the floor.

"Look," Lyle says. "The CA's office is gonna suspend disposition if you plead out. You're guilty now, then in six months they'll drop the charge so long as you don't get arrested in the meantime. It's like probation, only your record's wiped at the end."

A clean record means going back to work, getting on with life. Maybe start saving again to fly west.

"When can I go back to substituting?" I ask Lyle. "I need back on the list."

He gives me a blank look. He hasn't thought this through. "I guess when your record's expunged in six months?"

Jesuseffinchrist.

"But like, why are we pleading guilty? We weren't actually doing anything, man," BG says to Lyle. Says it sharp, in the voice that only siblings can get away with.

"This is a good deal, dude. No jail time. No record. The cops say you were lying in wait under the bleachers. They've got screenshots from Instagram. All that day. Travis threatening that he and his crew were gonna, and I quote, royally fuck the victim up."

"That's us?" BG responds. "His crew?"

We've never been anybody's crew. Figures the first time anyone decides we are, it's just so they can throw us in jail.

"We had Slurpees," I say. "Who brings a Slurpee to jump somebody?" Should I have saved my Slurpee cup as evidence? I'm not sure how any of this works.

"Where's Trav?" BG asks. But Travis has a felony charge and was direct-indicted to Circuit Court, one level up.

"Look," Lyle explains. "The CA understands Travis was the problem, but she says y'all were his lackeys. Says they got you cold and this is the best you're gonna do. Or we can roll the dice and go to trial. They got witnesses."

We don't have witnesses. Not even Trav, not that he could or would take the fall for this. But what is a witness gonna say? That we were sitting there, sipping menacingly?

"I didn't do anything," I explain to Lyle, calmly, though he flinches a bit as I do it. "Literally nothing. How're they supposed to put me in jail beyond a reasonable doubt for having a Slurpee with some dickwad who lost his shit on someone?"

"To win this," Lyle continues, "we'd have to prove you weren't gathered with Travis for the purpose of committing violence. And with the Instagrams, that doesn't look good." I glance at BG and can see his resolve slipping.

"Instagram? I'm not even on Instagram. And if I kicked your ass and said Jesus told me to, does that make Jesus guilty?"

"Depends. Was Jesus with you when you did it?"

God, Lyle is such a smartass.

"We don't even know Travis!" I say, losing my shit a little.

"They say you do."

"I just work with him," says BG.

"And I guess he's my cousin of some sort."

"Plus we went to school with his sister," BG adds.

"Why were you waiting under the bleachers?" Lyle asks, being a dumbass. He's asked this question before.

"Why the hell do you do anything when you're drunk?" BG shouts, loud enough the bailiff has to shush him. It prompts a few gavel bangs. I'm beginning to see how this might not go well in front of a judge.

"Next time I see Travis, I'm gonna teabag the shit out of him," I mutter.

Lyle winces again, as if he's worried I'll do it. As if it's possible. As if I'm not 5'6" and 140 pounds with scoliosis and a crooked elbow. As if I'm not broke and lonely and afraid of everything. As if I don't have a crush on a Saint Bernard of a man that happens to be his little brother, the one I've known for ten years who'll answer his phone at two in the morning and drive all the way over the mountain to pick me up when I'm drunk after striking out with college boys at Charlottesville's only gay bar, and then drive me back the next day so I can retrieve my truck.

Lyle says he'll give us a minute to think about it.

We don't have to do much thinking. BG tells me he's going to take the deal. I tell him I won't, that I can beat this at trial. I haven't done shit in my life and I'm not about to start by pleading guilty for it. But I can tell BG understands. We look at each other in silence for a few minutes and he gives me a strong hug. My cheek in his collarbone. First time I've felt okay all day.

When we wave Lyle back over and tell him our plan, his face falls. No hiding his exasperation. "Guys. That's not how it works. The Commonwealth doesn't want to do the work of trying this case, that's why they're offering the deal. If one of you goes to trial, you both have to."

BG looks at me. "Whatever you want," he says. He doesn't mean it.

The CA comes over. She speaks to Lyle as if we're not there. "Your guys ready?"

Lyle looks at me too, waiting for an answer.

I don't want anything bad to happen to me. Most of all I don't want anything bad to happen to BG.

The thing they don't tell you about taking a plea deal is it takes thirty seconds to let the prosecutor know, and forever waiting for it to be entered into judgment. Nothing to do but think in between. When we're finally called, the judge asks us a million dumb questions in a million dumb ways: Do you know what plead means? Do you know what guilty means? Do you know this waives your right to appeal? Do you assert you are pleading this free of coercion or threat? They wait for us to say yes to each one, and then find us guilty, disposition suspended for six months. I thought there would be some relief when it was over, but my stomach sinks with the gavel bang. The victim is standing next to the CA, staring at us the whole time from his purple polo. His face has healed pretty good.

Judge finally done, the bailiff leads us out through a side door up a dank stairway to the clerk's office. We wait at the window there for another forever as the ladies get our paperwork together. I can see the coffeemaker on the other side, like a taunt. When the papers are ready, the clerk hands me a bill for $413.00. Court costs, she tells me. Will I be paying credit or do I have the cash on hand?

I don't have the money. She gives me a canned lecture and a grace period till the first of the month.

"What the fuck are court costs?" I ask Lyle when I see him in the parking lot.

"Oh yeah," he says. "Don't forget to pay those. They aren't kidding around—they'll suspend your license. And don't get cute if they do—they got these scanners on the cop cars now that tell them if a car's owner lost their license. Bust you for sure."

"Lyle, I don't have four hundred bucks."

He shrugs. "Most of the folks locked up in County are in for driving suspended."

I'm simmering. "You didn't tell me about court costs."

"Well I'm doing you guys pro bono. It's cheaper than what I woulda charged you."

"Not cheaper than a public defender who would've let me say no to the deal."

Lyle gets pissed at this. Fair. I know he's here for free, trying to help. I'm not sure who I'm allowed to be mad at. My anger needs a destination.

I look at BG, who is standing behind his brother, as if he's reverted to childhood.

"I'm sorry man. Not like I have the money for mine either," he says.

"I just wouldn't've taken the deal if I'd known about this."

"I said I'm sorry," he says, scanning the ground. "I'm sorry for getting us into this mess. For talking to Travis in the goddamn 7-Eleven."

"You always say sorry for the wrong shit. You should be sorry for making me take the deal."

"Fuck you," says BG, sharp and hard, a wounded howl. He tells me he didn't make me take anything. That I had my own free will. That I had a million chances to change my mind, especially when the judge asked all those questions. I scrunch up my face because all that's true, but it's not the *truth* truth.

The truth truth is BG's full of shit. He knows why. Knows there's no saying it out loud. That I would never be able to say no when he wanted a yes. That's the way we work. That's why he likes us, likes knowing I'll never leave. Knows he'll never have to feel alone. But it's a shitty way to be a friend, I want to tell him. I want to scream it to him. To tear him apart until he wraps his arms around me. But I don't. I can't.

I turn around and walk back to my truck, through the thin crowd of grocery shoppers. A mother walking her kid to the store on a leash. Six firefighters in blue T-shirts stocking up the station house. An old couple squabbling about buying milk, too much or not enough.

When I get in my truck, I slam the door. There is no one to do it, but I want to be held.

In the sudden quiet of driving home alone, I'm so tired I'm afraid I'll nod off. As if to save me, David calls from California. He's driving too, says he's going into work at the winery. Says the sky is orange, not from sunrise but from smoke. They're under a pre-evacuation order, though he doesn't seem all that busted up about it.

"I'll get moving soon as they tell me to," he says. "You know me."

I don't really, but I know better than to say so. Talking feels weird, forced.

"Stay safe, man. Mom's really freaked," I tell him. But it's not Mom that's in trouble. "You scared?" I add.

"A little, always," David says, which surprises me. Then he asks if I'm all right.

"Yeah, sorry about the text. Shit worked itself out." It's half-true. I have no idea how I'm gonna get a hold of four hundred dollars in the next three weeks. But I'm not in jail.

"You should come visit. When the fires are done. Lots of guys to introduce you to."

"Yeah," I say, and mean it. "If California's still there."

BG is calling on the other line. It takes everything I have, but I don't pick up. I'd rather see Travis than BG at this point. And if

I ever see Travis again, I'm gonna run him over with my truck.

I head back to Mom's. There's the cat to feed. Plants to overwater. I park in the carport. Her spot, not that she's coming home to mind. Still, it takes me a minute to get up and go into the house. I just sit awhile in the cab, gathering. Part of me would do this all day. No one's around to notice.

MIDDLE DISTANCE
Matt W. Miller

Some drizzling day you'll drive down a road
    you'd not been on since you were twenty-two

and tawny, sleeveless, behind a forty-eight
    inch Scag, jeans and boots dusty with August,

a fatty of Cope between your lip and gums,
    and nothing to your mind but the long lines

you've made and all the lines yet left to mow
    in a sprawl of yards around a sprawl of homes.

You'll almost hear Mitch, the boss, bark at a stoned
    Sean balding edges with a string trimmer

and recall the end of another day, legs long beyond
    ache, hands soft calloused by rakes and just the sky

and grass and the dull eternal gas engine growl.
    Seventy yards and another turn, another

true line, pivot, verse and reverse, until
    the rhythm will sputter on some kids' toys left out

in the back. Toys you have to stop to move—
    beach pails, bubble wands, trucks, a tricycle—

toys you think even your own kids have long moved past.
    You'll realize you walked every inch of that grass,

more even than whoever lived there then.
    Or lives there now. And now, well down the road,

you'll see the dandelion you pulled from a bed
   of hemlock late that baking Friday afternoon,

the sun sagging its belly on the tickling pines,
   a rewilding world you cut from the bloom.

OUR OWN THIEVERY

Jed Myers

The bed squealed on us to the shadows
of our getaway. We whispered, laughed,
and let the daylight's inquest go on
delivering its indictments to the trees,

the rooftops, the glass towers, tent-dwellers
working the ramps, all the bright hulls
drifting the blacktop canals—the sun's
floodlight on the easy evidence, while we lay

low in our cove. Sure, we noticed
the curtains, shifty in the open window.
We overheard that soft flip-flop
testimony of the fabric on frame and sash.

Hints of wind reached in like the murmurs
of a courthouse crowd. The air knew
where to find us. But why now do I spin it
this way? We'd made off with the timeless

gem of an hour, till the light fell
and a chill slipped in. We were even granted
a sweet release, and when we walked
from each other after, it felt like free will.

So, let the record show we'd done nothing:
nothing, though while entangled together
we'd heard the volcanic dad two doors down
erupting again—we'd gone on

teasing sighs and moans and simple words
from each other. Had we registered
any of those sirens that kept calling
out of the University District? We hadn't

thought the loose fence slat's slaps could be
gunfire down there. Well, look at us,
in no way impaired, just heartsick
with our own thievery—we stole the day,

licking the light off each other's shoulders.
We'd siphon the stars down our throats.

PAJAMA MAN

Kevin McWilliams Coates

Pajama Man rules the neighborhood from the White House, flannel in any weather. When it is cold, he tugs the sleeves of his pajamas down farther over his wrists; when it is hot, he leaves only the top button done and we see his pasty, white-haired belly. Pajama Man lives in the White House at the top of the hill with trim lawns that he edges himself and round marigolds like egg yolks under the big picture window. He picks up snails and throws them into the street where we collect them into mayonnaise jars. We think Pajama Man could be president, could be a millionaire, but instead he lives on our street. We watch his house every day from our bikes, one foot on the ground and the other on a pedal, ready to ride away.

Our mother comes to our front steps and yells, "Jannery," a rough combination of Janice and Jerry, "come in the house now."

"Come in the house," echoes Pete the mynah bird from the open upstairs window. Our dad bought him used, not knowing that he was a cusser.

"He cusses a blue streak," our mother had protested to our dad. In his art book, Jerry draws a black bird with a blue lightning bolt coming out of his mouth. On it he writes all the bad words he knows—all the ones Pete says. When Pete hears our mother repeat herself, he gets frantic. We hurry toward home before he hears our mother's voice again.

"Come in the house now," yells our mother, and I wince.

"Goddamnit, goddamnit to hell," screams Pete. "What the hell? Jiminy Christmas!"

Pajama Man's front door is open just a crack, just enough that we think he might have heard. We cannot offend Pajama Man. Jerry and I go into my closet and have confession.

Jerry puts an old pair of Dad's boxers on his head, upside down, the elastic like a tiara and the legs like Dumbo ears. I slide a white, holey pair of Dad's athletic socks up over my hands past my elbows. We sit cross-legged facing each other, our arms stretched out straight in front of us, fingers touching. "Forgive us, Pajama Man, for we have sinned." We say it six times, a magic number; our dad has been gone for six months.

"Come to dinner," our mother calls, and we hide our artifacts again in the overnight bag that our dad did not take. Our mother calls it a make-up case.

"It's too big for that," I tell Jerry. "She doesn't have that much make-up." I want it to be a suitcase, one he didn't need.

"He didn't take it because he's not just gone for overnight," Jerry says.

"Buy a Ford," screams Pete, and Jerry and I stop to listen.

Pajama Man is walking to the mailbox at the bottom of his stairs. We watch from behind his front hedge. As he flips through the mail, he says things over and over. "Again, again, again," he says. "Again, again." And then, "Not again, not again. For her— for me—for me."

For her? We have never seen a Pajama Woman. Is she dead? Did she leave Pajama Man the way our dad left our mom, bags packed and yelling?

"Don't be silly," says Jerry. "No one would ever leave Pajama Man."

I hope with my fingers crossed and my toes crossed that our dad has written a letter to me and mailed it to Pajama Man's house so our mother wouldn't get upset. Maybe he'll tell me where he is. Maybe he wants me to join him. It used to be balanced: a dad, a mom, two kids. Now everything is off: a mom and mom's "little man" and me. I don't fit. Will Dad write to me? I think about this long enough that it becomes reasonable and likely.

I step out from behind the hedge. "Did you get any letters for me?" I call to Pajama Man. Jerry covers his eyes, sits down lower.

Pajama Man turns and looks at me. He pretends not to know who I am. "What do you want?" he yells.

From our upstairs window, Pete yells back, "Come on in! Buy a Ford."

"Did you get any letters for me?" I ask again.

He looks at me for a long time, then turns and walks back up his stairs, saying over and over but not to my face, "What do you want? What do you want?"

After he shuts his door, Jerry pulls me back behind the hedge and wipes away my tears with hands still wet with his own.

"Pajama Man can't tell you," he says to me. "Pajama Man just gives us signals. We have to figure it all out. He's not supposed to tell us anything."

Pajama Man is our religion this summer. I reach out to take communion, and Jerry receives our commandments in his dreams. The blessed mother hides in the kitchen, no room at the inn.

When it rains and we can't go outside, Jerry and I scour our house for signs. We have checked all the dresser drawers, the medicine cabinet, the closets. We make lists of what our dad took with him and what he left. It is a mystery, a puzzle. We have to find the clues and then watch Pajama Man for signs.

"He did not take any of his tools," I say, adding 'tools' to the paper headed, THINGS LEFT. "He did not take any books."

"But he did take," says Jerry, writing on the THINGS TOOK list, "his lawn-mowing sneakers and his transistor radio."

"Not his umbrella. Not his high school letter jacket."

"Yes on sunglasses."

We believe that everything we have lost in these last six months has disappeared with our dad: the new box of crayons, Jerry's old wristwatch, the cat's collar. Those missing things seem to be the important things, like those missing people always seem to be the important ones.

I find our mother sitting in a kitchen chair and crying.

"What's wrong?" I ask. "Why are you crying?" I want to ask: How long will this take? What comes next?

"I'm not crying," is all she says to me.

Jerry and I play catch with an old tennis ball in front of Pajama Man's house. We throw and catch easily, native rhythm like a ritual in our hearts. Is he watching? He is digging in his perfect flowerbed. Jerry is counting our catches, I can tell, his mouth mutely tallying like a litany. He counts so hard he misses, the ball tipping off his fingers into the backyard over Pajama Man's fence.

We walk solemnly up to Pajama Man. He is pretending not to

have seen us or our ball.

"Excuse me, please," Jerry says, "but our ball went over your fence. Can I get it back?"

Pajama Man looks first at me and then at Jerry. When we don't move, he says, "What do you want?"

"Our ball, please," Jerry says. "It went in your backyard. Can I get it back?"

Pajama Man's face starts to light up like he is receiving divine intervention, but then he scowls. He stands up, rubbing the dirt from his hands on his pajama thighs.

"Go use your own bathroom!" he yells loud enough that Pete hears.

"Come on in," answers Pete.

"You go home," he yells into Jerry's face, "and use your own bathroom!"

"Goddamnit!" answers Pete. "Come on in, goddamnit!"

And Jerry, because he is a good boy, an obedient boy, a small man playing by all of the rules he can discover—Jerry goes home and goes to the bathroom. I am alone with Pajama Man.

He watches Jerry run home and then says to me, "What do you want?" But now his voice is quieter. "What do you want?"

I cannot answer in words. All I want right now is to sit on this orderly, neat lawn and get rid of any snails, to go inside the house Pajama Man never leaves, to touch the worn flannel of his pajamas. I want to be eaten alive by the religion of Pajama Man.

Pajama Man is standing at his front window, the curtains open just enough to make room for his whole body. Jerry and I stand in our driveway and look up at him. He pretends not to see us.

We walk two houses down to Bryce and Brett's house. Bryce is my age and Brett is two years younger, like Jerry, so it works like a machine. When they see us coming, they get their record player from the shelf and plug it in on the hearth. They know to put on the *Alvin and the Chipmunks* record. As it starts, we go in a circle in this order: me, Bryce, Jerry, Brett. We walk in a lilting march, in a solemn prance, in a circle again and again. When the first side is over, we turn the record to Side Two and start again.

If we slow down the record, Alvin, Theodore, and Simon sound like adults. We push gently on the needle arm until it drags and slows, and then we contemplate it. Are their real voices the chipmunk ones we have managed to make adult, or are their real voices the grownup ones they have managed to make young? We all know they are not real chipmunks.

When the record is over, both sides, we sit down where we ended up in the march.

"So," says Brett, "what do you guys want to do?"

Jerry and I want to stay here at their house. It is a perfect copy of our house, room for room, only the furniture is different. It feels exotic, like someone's underwear drawer is open, like it is a parallel universe.

"We want to watch your dad come home," says Jerry.

"That's not for a long time," Bryce says, looking at me.

"We'll wait," I say, and we put on Side One of *Alvin* again.

Bryce and Brett's mom gives us apple slices and Kool-Aid. She looks us right in our eyes—me, then Jerry, then me again—and puts her hands on my cheeks. She stands this way a long time, and finally says, "How is your mother?"

"I haven't seen her for a while," I answer. I wish she would ask us about our dad, but I haven't seen him for even longer.

Jerry rescues me. "Our mom found an Easter egg today," he tells her. "Blue. It was in the little drawer in the china cabinet. No Easter bunny would be dumb enough to leave one where no one would ever look."

"Did she eat it?" asks Brett.

"No, dummy," Jerry says. "Of course not. It was rotten. She only found it because it smelled so bad."

"Our dad hid it," I tell them all. "He knew we'd find it, but not until he'd been gone a while. It was like a present."

"A present of an egg?"

Jerry and I are very sure.

When their dad finally does come home, Brett runs to him and shouts, "Did you bring me an egg?" He lifts Brett up and kisses him on the neck, then Bryce, and then Jerry steps forward, so their dad lifts him for a neck kiss, too.

The mom says, "Oh, Ed," and pats my shoulder so I know I will not be getting a neck kiss. I want one, want to smell the good daddy smell of sweat, city air, onion, and after-shave all mixed together. This is not how Pajama Man smells.

When we go home, Pete is screaming so loud and so long that our mother has closed all the windows, like she used to do when our dad still lived here. She is not happy. "Where have you been?" she asks us.

"Down the street," I tell her.

"I called for you."

"Come on in, goddamnit to hell," screams Pete. He says it in the low voice of the man who used to own him. When he says, "Dinnertime," it is with my mother's voice.

"Didn't you hear me call?" she asks me. Jerry is looking at Pete, listening to him and heading for the closet.

"Yes, I heard you," I lie. "I just didn't recognize your voice."

For dinner we have bright orange macaroni and cheese and canned peaches. "Can I make my milk orange, too?" asks Jerry, and our mother starts, again, to cry.

Pajama Man's house at night has only one light on at a time. We sit at my window upstairs and watch him move from room to room. I have taught Jerry to bite into the wooden windowsill. We bite, move down, bite, move down, the length of the sill. It is covered by about four layers of different colors of enamel from beige at the bottom up to a pale yellow. I want it to be plain white, bright white, but our mother can't paint the house all by herself.

We watch him go from the living room to his upstairs bedroom, the dim lights turned on only in those rooms. It's hard to make out the kitchen, and we can't see a bathroom, so we are unsure if he goes into those rooms ever, at least at night. Our mother walks in as we are singing our dad's lullaby to Pajama Man.

"How come," I ask her, "our house and Bryce and Brett's house and all the other houses on this street are the same except for his?"

She comes to the window and looks where I point up to the White House in the streetlights. She puts her finger to the glass; if there were no glass, she would be touching Pajama Man's front curtains. "But it is," she tells me, and I hear Jerry's sharp intake of breath and then the sound of him biting down, hard. "It's exactly the same as ours except he painted it all white. Siding, stucco, all of it is white." She kisses each of us on the top of our heads and leaves before we can ask another question.

Jerry is too young to go to school with me. Bryce and I walk off down the street alone. Brett stands on his front porch and yells as we turn the corner, "Come back, Baby," because that was what he called Bryce before he could say Bryce. Jerry stands on our matching front porch and salutes.

I sit behind a curly-haired boy who smells like food I have never eaten. He traces his letters at least four times each until the pencil marks smudge together and the paper is a gray mess like dried paper mache. The teacher holds his paper up because it is such a mess. The boy looks down at the pencil in his fist, and I think I love him.

But all of the girls are supposed to love Gregory Peterson because he has blond hair, white-blond like the hairs on Pajama Man's stomach. He is the one we chase. When I catch hold of his sweater, he looks at me with eyes so light blue they are almost like snow.

I get stomachaches from going to school. My teacher is named either Mrs. Bien or Mrs. Biem, and I have never seen anyone with hair so dark and straight. All of her blouses button all the way up on her neck. I cannot remember whether to call her Mrs. Biem or Mrs. Bien. One time when I say her name out loud, Gregory Peterson tells me I used a bad word, the grownup word for poop. But which was it, Bien or Biem? I can't remember, so I stop raising my hand in class. I start to cry whenever she asks me anything. She calls our mother to the school.

When she comes home from talking to my teacher, our mother looks tired. She hands me a small plastic jar of mints. She says the green ones are for when I'm a little sad, the yellow ones are for when I might start crying, and the pink ones are for when I'm already crying. I can take them to school.

I give Jerry one every day before I leave so he won't cry, and I make myself not cry at school by taking the yellow ones and drawing pictures of Pajama Man. My mother is happy her plan worked. I can't cry anymore, so I start having nosebleeds. There are no mints to put in my nose, so on those days I get to come home.

I teach Jerry how to read and how to trace over each of his letters repeatedly until the words look like a lost treasure map. I tell him that someday, to prove we love Pajama Man, we will have to chase him.

All the mothers on our street have decided to sew Ten Little Indian costumes for Halloween, and we will all trick-or-treat together. No one asked us, but there is the suede fabric and the loose colorful beads in a pile on our kitchen table, so it will be all right. It will be me, Jerry, Bryce, Brett, the young girl who lives next door to Pajama Man, three kids who live around the corner but we don't play with because they are too big, and two kids we don't know but whose moms know us. Jerry and I can hardly wait to knock on Pajama Man's door.

"He will open the door," Jerry says, "and we'll look quick inside."

"What will we see?" I ask.

"A ladder, I think," says Jerry. "And maybe some paint. A chair that goes up and down like in a dentist's office."

I wait.

"A solid silver table like for a throne, and a rug made of rabbit skin."

Each day, the longer I wait, the more Jerry tells me.

"Pictures on the wall like churches," he whispers. "And the candy he gives out on Halloween will be real chocolate from France."

When Halloween finally arrives, we are lined up by height, and Jerry and I stand three people apart. The other eight Little Indians march right on past the White House because no lights are on, so they think that Pajama Man is not at home. Jerry and I know better, know that he is in the back upstairs bedroom, pretending not to see us.

We don't want to share Pajama Man with any of these Little Indians anyway, but we do salute as we walk by.

The outdoor version of *Alvin and the Chipmunks* is on bikes. We all ride around and around in the circle in front of the White House. Jerry still has his training wheels, and he doesn't think they will ever come off. Our dad took mine off.

"He didn't take his tools," I say. But we have already been to the garage, have already held the plastic handles of screwdrivers and hammers, trying to feel any eroded indentations that prove his hand was here, any remnants of our dad's warmth.

"But even," he says, "if we figure out how to take them off," and we both figure we could do that, "there would be no one to hold me."

Our dad had held his hand on the back of my bicycle seat and had run behind me in Alvin circles. I could at first feel him, then I pretended to lose him. Then he lost me. I rode past Pajama Man's house, and there was our dad on the sidewalk, waving. I fell.

"But you got up," Jerry says, "and you rode again."

I have tried to run alongside Jerry as he rides, but I can't keep up, and I'm not strong enough to hold Jerry steady like our dad could have.

"Neither," says Jerry, working at the nuts that hold on his training wheels, "is our mom."

So Jerry rides at dusk around and around the circle when everyone else has gone inside. He rides, falls, rides, falls. It is his ritual; he teaches me, like I taught him how to bite the windowsill. I ride and jump off with him when he falls to give him courage.

Jerry crosses himself before each ride, what he calls the sign of the kite, and rides off into his abyss. While he teaches himself to ride without training wheels, I sit on the curb, our mother calls out our front window, and Pajama Man pretends not to notice the tire marks Jerry leaves in circles in front of his house.

At Christmastime our mother stands on a kitchen chair at the top of the stairs and opens the high attic door. She crawls in and hands down to us boxes of ornaments, lighter than they look. They are taped shut with tape that has the dust of our father's fingers. We peel it back.

Our same family as last year is still in the box: the Play-Doh stars and trees, the fancy beaded angel from when our mother was a girl, the blown-glass star Jerry gets to place at the top of the tree when our father lifts him up each year.

"He didn't take any ornaments," whispers Jerry, and I see in his eyes the hope he still holds tight to his body like those Christmas morning miracles. I know that those miracles are carefully stashed under the double bed with the maple bookshelf headboard in our mother's room; I have already looked there for our father but found only a few presents.

Jerry is pulling old newspaper from our family's nativity set. Our mother has been making it for years, and it is still not done. She uses scraps of old cloth and trimmings and junk jewelry to decorate old bottles into people. So far we have the blessed mother, a tall, slender wine bottle covered with linens and velvet. Baby Jesus is a tiny spice bottle, swaddled in cottons, the round stopper a baby halo. The angel has brocade and lace, an antique carafe with beveled sides. The kings are magnificent: dark rich brocades, gold braids, and jeweled clasps decorating fancy liqueur bottles.

"Shall we make a shepherd this year?" asks our mother. "I have an old glass milk bottle that is just humble enough."

"You can make a shepherd," says Jerry, "but me and Janice are going to make Joseph." Our mother and I look at Jerry, and he says, "The dad. We're going to make the dad."

This year we only have a tabletop tree. Our mother doesn't have enough money for a six-foot one. She puts a TV tray in the middle of the front window, covers it with a white sheet—"for snow," says our mother—and sets the little tree on that. Jerry doesn't even need a boost to get the star on the top. I think he will be proud, but instead he is grumpy and only picks a few ornaments to hang. We can't get the whole lot of our ornaments onto this little tree, so we pick the best ones. Jerry tires of this.

"I can't pick," he says. "The ones we don't pick will be so sad." He goes into the kitchen to find a bottle to make into the dad.

"There's a large vinegar one in the sink cupboard," sings out our mother as if everything is fine. "It has a good shape to it."

Jerry doesn't answer, but we hear him rummaging around.

"That tall Kahlúa one in the china cabinet is almost empty," she calls. "I could clean that out for you."

Jerry opens the refrigerator and stands in front of it without speaking for a few minutes.

"Don't let all the cold air out," our mother calls.

Jerry shuts the door and walks carefully back to us.

"This," he says, holding out a full beer bottle, "will be the dad."

Our mother goes quiet. Jerry acts like he doesn't notice.

"Our dad's the only one who ever drank beer, so it'll be perfect."

Our mother moves toward Jerry as if to hold him, but instead she reaches for the bottle. "I'll empty it down the sink," she says, "and wash it out for you."

"Don't you think it's kind of short?" I ask. I don't want Jerry to do this, don't want to see his patched-together, childish Joseph next to the perfect angel, the rich kings.

"No," he says and backs up. "It's perfect like it is. Full." Our mother stops moving toward him.

"But Jerry," she says, "that beer won't last forever. It'll go bad; it'll turn rotten."

"Like the egg," I say.

Jerry smiles. "Just like the egg," he says, looking at me. "A present."

For who? I want to ask. Instead I go to the sink cupboard and get the vinegar bottle. It has a skinny neck and a round belly. I go to our mother's scrap bag and find what I want: flannel scraps. I will create the real one who's missing. I will create Pajama Man.

And I will make him talk.

All the department store Santas have Pajama Man's eyes, his belly. We think they could be our father behind the fake beards and the suits.

"What do you want?" they ask us, echoing Pajama Man, as we settle onto a lap. We wonder if he'll have a good daddy smell. "What do you want?"

"We already wrote you a letter," says Jerry, not fooled for a single minute but hoping. "Don't you remember what it said?"

"Do you have any idea how many letters I get?" answers the Santa. "Do you have any idea how many little boys there are in the world?"

"No," says Jerry. "How many?"

The Santa shifts his weight beneath our oppressive needs. "That's not the issue," he says. "Just tell me what you want."

We want to order all the things that are missing at our house. We want to order more mints to stem our tears. Easter eggs. Onion and sweat and after-shave. But the Santa gets tired of waiting for our answer and bends down to his sack. He hands each of us a candy cane.

"This," says Jerry, waggling it back in the Santa's face, "is not what I asked for."

"It's all anyone can do," says the Santa, and I pull Jerry away.

We pool our allowances and spend our money on Christmas candles from the grocery store, one shaped like an angel for our mother and one a naked snowman to give to Pajama Man. Jerry wants to get a Santa one for our dad, but I say no.

"Here is why," I tell him. "First the angel will lose her head and then her wings; the snowman will melt without a sound. Santa will sit spiteful under the tree until he is a sore spot in our eyes, until he is as rotten as an old Easter egg. Instead, we'll save our money and go to a pay phone to find our dad on the day after Christmas." I pretend I have received a sign.

Jerry, the original dreamer, makes the sign of the kite and looks past Christmas.

The morning after Christmas, we go outside. I see the wrapped box with the snowman candle still on Pajama Man's porch, and I hope Jerry doesn't see it, but of course he does. I think he will be upset, will think it is a bad sign, but he doesn't. He says, "That is so polite. He's waiting to open it until we talk to our dad." Jerry is sure.

We walk to the pay phone at the grocery store and look in the phone book for a minute until I realize it's an old phone book and it won't know anything. I call Information.

"I need the number of our dad," I say, and I tell the operator his name. When she starts to read me a number, I smile, but then I hear the number she is saying.

"No," I tell her, "that's my phone number. I want his new number."

"A new listing?" she asks.

I say yes, but I am wishing I could sit down a minute. I don't know how new is new. Ten months is a long time to me.

"Sorry, nothing under that name," she says.

"You're wrong!" I tell her. "He moved to a new place, and he has to have a phone. Why can't you find it?"

I hear her exhale. "Is it possible," she asks me, "that he is in another town? Do you want me to check another town?"

Until this moment I have not considered that our dad could ever be that far away.

"Or maybe," she says, "he's with friends, maybe I could try another name?"

I have also not pictured our dad with anyone but us: not a new wife, not with other dads, just totally and completely alone. I realize that I don't know anything.

Jerry hangs up the phone for me, and we go home. At our driveway, Jerry looks up at the White House and sees our box still there. He runs up the street, and I follow. He goes up the steps, picks up the box, and knocks hard at the front door.

When Pajama Man opens it, we can feel heat from the fireplace inside his house. Pajama Man looks at Jerry and then at me, but it is me he asks, "What do you want?"

Jerry pushes the box into Pajama Man's stomach, and he has to take it in both of his flannel hands. He looks at me again, the box held at his waist, and says again to me, "What do you want?"

Jerry screams at him, "Just go to the bathroom! Use your own bathroom!"

As he continues to scream this, over and over, I hear Pete answer from our house, "Goddamnit to hell! Get in here! Buy a Ford, goddamnit!"

When he turns to go back inside, the box in his hands, I see a damp patch on his flannel back, like a map of the world I can't understand, a stream of sweat down his neck like the only highway out of here.

Jerry and I look for snow out the bedroom window every day, but it has never snowed where we are. The air pushes against the window like a threat. Jerry and I go into our closet when we're tired of standing right over the heater vent, but Jerry won't do confession anymore. Instead, he takes our dad's old boxers and works his fingers to tear and poke little holes in them. I sit with our dad's socks in my lap like they are kittens, petting them to sleep.

Jerry looks me right in the eye. "It's almost a year," he says, his voice flat and powerful like an anvil. "He's never coming back."

"He's gone forever?" I ask.

"Forever," he says. He stands and looks down at me from a huge distance. "We need to grow up."

A siren comes up the street like punctuation, and we see flashing red lights pass our window. Pete screams, "Come on in," in our mother's voice.

We go outside and up the street to see the ambulance at Pajama Man's curb. In a minute several men bring out a stretcher with the big vinegar bottle shape of Pajama Man on it. I think maybe he's been wearing pajamas forever just waiting for this day, so he won't have to change at the hospital. His eyes are half-open as we watch him be carried by, and as his eyes brush past, pretending not to see me, I say, "What do you want?"

The ambulance door is closed, and they drive him down the street. To another town? To live with friends?

We wait for everyone to go back into their houses. Jerry looks up at me and says, "Grow up," not unkindly.

"You grow up," I say right back.

"Let's get our ball," he says, heading for Pajama Man's yard, for a world I can't understand, on the only highway out of here.

STATE OF SORRY

Julia Edwards

My mother and I drive to the Blue Ridge mountains
listening to Bruce Springsteen and the fruit stand
in the flash rain becomes the last thing you said to me,

its red soggy arteries. I turn the song up, *oh, thunder
road, oh, thunder road* until I cannot feel myself turn
away from you shouting along with big helium eyes

last summer in the karaoke light. I look out at the range,
turning the furnace in my brain away from sorrow
level flames. *They're always blue*, says my mother

and it's true, they're beautiful—these massive hills.
On a hike, she reads the brochure of George Vanderbilt's
life—how he came here on doctor's orders, fell in love

with the landscape and died soon after he built his
empire. *All his focus on health didn't help him
in the end*, Mom explains and a passerby tells us

how silence cured her, expanding from her ears into
the lake. I hear a piercing when I hesitate so I apologize
for the noise we do not have in common. After you

died, my mother said *depression* and I hear myself
count the letters in goodbye—their shrinking. I want
to tell you how I'm filled with defunct rage, a gutted

socket people flick their sorry matches out in. I want
to tell you thunder gives me a false sense of shape
but I am stuck in a state of windless need. Give me

your most electric morning, brand me warm like
the cold Biltmore horses. Give me your silence
but don't let me keep it. *Show a little faith,*

there's magic in the night. I dream of setting fire
to the barn where goats lay sleeping. Not one
wakes for me to tell him, *hey, it's alright.*

ANOTHER OLD BIRD FLIES ACROSS THE RIVER

K.R. Segriff

Doris of the frozen roast hurled
at the son-of-a-bitch in the produce aisle
who talked shit about Gramps.

Doris of the palm-tree nails creeping
across her buried spine, as she recalls
the sensation of touching bone.

Doris of the chartreuse bedroom painted
a shade Gramps despised while he was off
in Verdun with god-knows-who.

Doris of the late August veranda, sizzling
her skin so dark that all the old hens
whispered into their teacups.

Doris of the 1940s photograph, teeth crossed, posed
between Gramps and the mighty Saint Lawrence,
thinking, even then, of shoving him in.

Doris of the long drive home from the hospital.
The strawberry, honey, and juniper infused evening.
The lingering scent of gin and grief.

Now, Doris of the feet-first exit.

Doris of the torn heart valve.

Doris of the mile-wide, uneven smile.

Doris of the ambulance screaming past
the mighty Saint Lawrence.

Doris who whispered across the whitecaps
that Gramps better start swimming because, goddamnit,
she was coming in after him.

STRAY THINGS DO NOT CARRY A SOUL
Kanza Javed

Daddy worked many jobs, but Daddy liked his second job the best. He liked shooting stray dogs in streets the best.

Every morning Daddy swept the roads, painted dull pavements, and unclogged jammed gutters in Victoria Colony, and every evening, he slung the shotgun over his shoulder, left the servant quarters, and went into the dimming alleys looking for dogs. He told me it was okay to hunt them down because they were feral. Borderline mad. They were no one's anything. They had no mothers. No one wailed for them after they were gone. They were stray, and stray things did not carry a soul.

When November arrived, I dropped out of school, much to my mother and older sister's consternation, and began accompanying my father to work. My mother had been dreaming of a better future for me. One where I had a proper job. She did not want me raking leaves in a rich man's red-brick bungalow or playing cricket in the garden with his son who only spoke in English—she envisioned better things. Perhaps I could have been a well-dressed clerk at a government office, or an IT specialist in an English medium school like my mother's younger brother, Aslam. He had taken a computer training course after his BA exams.

"I don't shop at the landa bazaar now," he said on his last visit to our servant quarter. We were sitting on charpoys in the small open courtyard drinking chai. I noticed he was wearing a green and white plaid dress shirt.

Uncle Aslam was a big man now. "I shop at the mall. Never the flea market again."

Mother liked her brother's new extravagance. She watched him prosper with fascination. It was something she had never been granted growing up—a chance to dwell, leap, prosper, make mistakes, fix them, and leap again. A chance to find herself and find out what she was good at besides squatting and sweating profusely before a gas stove, making parathas and fenugreek leaves and potatoes. Mother had many resentments.

Mother was married off at fifteen to a distant cousin, my father, who lived in the same village in Hafizabad. Both never attended school. Mother was a liability, and she would say that liabilities in her family were not sent to schools or colleges, but were bundled up and wedded off to cousins who worked or old widowers who needed young brides for their supper and ailing bodies.

Daddy told me he left school when he was seven because he didn't like his strict math teacher who hit students' palms with a wooden ruler when they got the multiplication table wrong. Daddy dashed back home one day, leaving behind his satchel and lunchbox on the school bench. It was lifting wheat sacks at a warehouse with his older brothers from then onward.

Mother had shoved Daddy out of the village to Lahore for a better life after they married. She had my sister, Rashda, at sixteen, lost five children after that (one died during birth, two strangled themselves in the womb, and two frail twins survived only a year), and then had me, a boy. A miracle child. Mother would say she had me after visiting various shrines, falling at the feet of many colorful saints, and after wearing multiple amulets.

"Mera beta," Amma would sing. "My beautiful little son. It was the big pir's prayer that blessed me with you, Haider Ali. Don't become a useless and soulless man like your father. Learn from your Uncle Aslam."

Daddy never cared for my uncle's new lifestyle, and did not like when he visited. Daddy didn't like his leather belts and shoes. He didn't like his ironed mall dress shirts, the rented two-room house, or his new wife who always wore a bright pink lipstick whenever she visited.

Once, Daddy and I watched Uncle Aslam speed away in his Honda CD 70 motorbike after telling us about his shopping mall trips. Daddy furrowed his eyebrows and spat in the open alley sewer outside the quarter. The narrow alley was strewn with servant quarters with tin doors, red spit stains, and cigarette butts.

"Sister-fucker," Daddy muttered in Punjabi.

If Uncle Aslam was a successful man, my father was a proud one.

I did not know who I wanted to be at the age of ten.

I did not know if I wanted to be like Uncle Aslam, whizzing and zooming through Lahore on my gleaming Honda, or to become like Daddy, with a pack of Morven cigarettes, ambling through colonial bungalows with jasmine vines and Rangoon creepers on walls, and holding a broom for sweeping or a thick bamboo stick for blocked drains and gutters.

What I did know was that I wanted a life somewhat similar to the one the little boy in Bungalow 17 had.

He was seven.

He had a blue bicycle which he rode around the circular driveway of the colonial house, went to school in a huge black car with a green government number plate, and called his father "daddy."

My father had taken me to Bungalow 17 several times. He was a part-time worker there. He washed the driveway, helped the gardener trim the hedges, and had lunch in the kitchen with the driver, Samander Khan.

The mistress needed extra help around the house and was looking for an errand boy, so my father took me there one day and offered my services.

The mistress stood on the porch wrapped up in a black shawl with red embroidered flowers and looked down at me. She asked why I wasn't at school.

"How can a poor man like myself pay for two kids' school?" my father began. "And my son says he doesn't want to go to school either."

"The driver said you've an older daughter too," she said. "Does she go to school?"

"Yes madam. She's sixteen. She's sitting for her matriculation exams in May."

"I can pay for the boy's expenses if he goes to school," the madam offered, looking down at me. I could tell from her face that she was impressed by my sister and a little disappointed in me.

Jealousy stirred in me. I felt about Rashda what my father felt about my uncle.

"Speak, boy." Daddy nudged me jokingly. "Would you go to school if sir pays?"

"I'd go to school if I could go in a big car like that." I pointed at the black Land Cruiser Samander Khan was cleaning.

Daddy smacked my head. The mistress chuckled and went in the bungalow through the screen door.

She had said I was hired.

That night, at dinner, neither my mother nor sister was too pleased with my new job at the big railway officer's bungalow. They were not enthralled by the five-bedroom house, the sprawling lush garden and backyard with pink bougainvillea and purple dahlias, or my salary of 2,000 rupees.

Daddy told them I was on a fast track to becoming a mard—a man. And if I continued working hard, I could soon buy a bicycle and a cell phone.

"Not a mard," Rashda said with her mouthful of red lentils and white rice. "A nakur."

Nakur.

A servant.

Mother cast Daddy a stern, unkind look. There was repugnance in her eyes. It was as if she accused him of her only son's failure. She looked at my father as if he were the bad seed in our family. The rotten apple. The corrupt, bad fish that could spoil the whole pond. She had said many times that if Daddy did not start bringing his entire salary home instead of spending it on other dangerous things, she would end up cleaning people's houses and washing clothes.

"This is your miracle child, Amma," Rashda derided. "Washing an officer's car and brooming dirty verandas. All that money you wasted for the three classes at school he barely passed."

Mother lifted the steel lid from the pressure cooker to pour lentils on her plate. Steam unfurled from the cooker and she disappeared behind the white fog. I was glad I could not see her disdain.

My sister meant every cruel, callous word she uttered.

We were both put in the same school in the crowded, humming Dharampura neighborhood near Victoria Colony. The lowly English medium school building with chipping white paint and growing gray-green mold was nestled between a meat market and a shop selling brassieres and whitening creams.

Rashda stayed in school and moved to its high school building. I gave up and fled. She said I couldn't make it because I was too stupid like all the illiterate men in our family. And there were many. Mother would count them on her fingers as examples for me.

Rashda's mockery made my body rattle with anger but I knew I had another way of getting back.

"Your husband is also a fifth fail," I reminded her. "He'll be a servant too and you'll also make rotis in his kitchen like Amma."

Rashda's smile drooped. She stopped eating and turned her troubled face away from me. I had aimed straight for the jugular.

She was betrothed to our cousin, Rehan, when she was only six—a common tradition in our family. A solemn pledge of child betrothal between solemn relatives at solemn hours, before a child comprehended her existence or distinguished amniotic fluid from Lahore's smoggy air.

I suspected my sister was interested in another boy who went to the evening tuition classes with her. I had caught a handwritten letter in one of her science practical books. I could not understand what it said, but there was a heart with an arrow drawn at the center of the writing. I had also seen her getting dropped off on a stranger's motorbike when Daddy was not around.

"It's my friend's brother," she clarified once. "I didn't have money for a rickshaw. Don't get stupid ideas."

"Get up." Daddy signaled for me to rise from the kitchen floor where I sat with my plate of rice. "Come with me."

He veered me away from the disappointed women to the courtyard and into the darkening alley outside. All the doors of the other servant quarters were shut. A Bollywood song played loudly on someone's television set. A group of young boys stood at the mouth of the alley smoking cigarettes and watching a video of a gyrating woman on a mobile phone.

Daddy and I walked around the colony in silence. There was repressed squeaking and twittering of birds and bats in old trees. I watched the suspended shotgun dance on Daddy's right shoulder as he fished out the pack of Morvens and matchbox from his pocket.

Other municipal marksmen did their work of shooting stray dogs in the afternoons or evenings, hours when the daylight had not yet slipped. And they did it when there was a complaint of a growing stray population in the streets or when there was a feral, mad dog trotting about, frightening bungalow women taking evening strolls.

Daddy liked the darkness, and he did not obey a time or an order for his shootings.

I noticed he liked to spend as little time at home as possible, probably because when he was outside, he could do whatever he liked. Be whatever he liked. The sweeper. The huntsman. My mentor. A friend. Someone important. At home, Amma ruled the roost.

Outside, Daddy had friends, and those friends always had gifts wrapped in small plastic pouches for him. I don't know what they contained but it made Daddy smile and firmly shake their hands. Daddy liked playing cards and betting crumpled 100 rupee notes in the quiet park near the mosque.

Daddy pulled the long shotgun off his shoulder and handed it to me. I held it, afraid, shakingly, in my arms like the gun was a sleeping baby. It was very heavy. He monitored my reluctance and grinned, displaying his deep red gums and decaying front teeth.

"It won't go off," he assured. "And it shouldn't go off because you don't have this."

He pulled out a plastic card from his front kameez pocket and proudly tapped at his signature on the Firearms License near his black-and-white photo.

I could tell he was proud he had a printed signature on the license instead of a thumbprint. He was not an angutha chaap—a jahil, an unlettered man who was asked to sign important documents with a thumb impression instead of a signature.

Daddy came closer to me and said that he was also an important man like Uncle Aslam, no matter what *Daddy's wife* said. Would the government hand an *unimportant man* a shotgun and assign him the task of saving lives from mad, feral things?

"Bilkul nahe." He shook his head, replying to his own question. "Your mother doesn't know anything. She just has a sharp tongue. A good woman doesn't talk too much."

He often said things like that when we were alone. He would say the same thing about Rashda too, that she had also begun talking too much.

I teetered after him with the gun. Daddy raised his hand, asking me to be still and stay back.

It was not time to shoot the dogs yet.

Once, I had asked one of Daddy's friends why they had to shoot the dogs in the city instead of just scaring them away.

"Do you know what happened to Chacha Rashid's youngest daughter?" Nisar replied.

Nisar was a butcher in the market near my old school. He sold sickly white chickens during summer months, and displayed thawed Rahu fish in winter.

I was sitting with him, Daddy, and an old man in the park, watching them gamble and play cards.

"Three dogs attacked the poor child," Nisar continued. "They couldn't find the rabies injection anywhere. There was foam coming from her mouth when she died the same night."

"Last summer, another dog bit a sleeping woman's arm," the old man spoke up. "Her arm was dangling from the charpoy. These feral dogs are not afraid of humans like they were before. They have developed a taste for human flesh."

"Do they also go to heaven or hell?" I asked. "These stray dogs?"

"No one waits for them in heaven or hell," said Daddy. "No one wants them in the afterlife either."

The three men reassured me that it was necessary to hunt and shoot. I had asked only because I'd grown quite fond of a black-and-white dog that lived in the scaffoldings of a construction site near Bungalow 17. A few times, I'd tossed him roti and bone, leftovers from my lunch in the bungalow kitchen.

There was a black fur spot on the dog's white back that was shaped like a dil. A heart. Like the one in Rashda's letter.

Daddy left me standing under a dim white streetlight with the shotgun. He disappeared behind a kikar tree. I could see that there were two other unfamiliar men waiting for him there.

I had seen Daddy do that many times, vanish behind a tree with his friends. In early mornings especially before he headed to work and late evenings before he began the culling spree. He would vanish behind a tree and resurface after a few long minutes without a word. I never asked him anything when he would return.

From the corner, I caught scraps of the affair. There was a man

STRAY THINGS DO NOT CARRY A SOUL

tying a strap on Daddy's bare arm. The other cracked a loud joke in Punjabi as he held a syringe. I saw Daddy's arms get heavy. He leaned his back against the tree. The rest of the scene was submerged in silence and shadows.

Dry leaves crunched under the men's feet.

A dog barked at a distance.

After some time the men dawdled away, leaving me with Daddy who took the shotgun from my arms. He stood still for a few minutes, playing with the loose bullets in his pocket. They made low-pitched clinks as he fidgeted.

"Do you hear them?" His words slurred a little. He was looking at a distance, listening intently to something.

More nameless, unwanted dogs barked and howled around the colony.

"Talking, barking, talking, barking. Do you hear them, Haider Ali?"

I did.

"Yapping away like those women at home."

Daddy was angry. He loaded the chamber with four bullets, cupped the barrel of the gun and pulled it toward himself. Something clicked. He meandered in the direction of the sounds.

I followed and watched Daddy aim at a pack of dogs rummaging through a garbage dump. They did not seem mad or dangerous. He signaled me to remain hushed and cover my ears. He shot two bullets.

There were sounds of whining and scurrying. A bullet took down a brown dog. Daddy aimed and shot at it again. The lifeless body jolted and remained as it was, lifeless. Quiet. But there was blood splatter the second time. The road was stained red.

"It's dead," I said loudly, my hands still covering my ears. "Why did you shoot it again?"

"We should be sure. Sometimes they don't die that easily."

I looked at the dead dog for some time. I could feel Daddy's eyes on me. I knew if I cried, he would call me *Na-mard*. He would tell me that I was not man enough. I was a eunuch or a little girl.

My body tingled. I thought I saw the dead dog quiver. Daddy said it did not and then we moved on, looking for dogs.

There was another difference between other colony marksmen

and my father. They had become part-time shooters to feed their families in the servant quarters. Fifty rupees per dead dog, Nisar and the old man had told me. But Daddy, Daddy enjoyed the morbid task. He enjoyed loading the shotgun and asking me to cover my ears. He enjoyed aiming and watching the dog tremble, fall, not dead, nearly dead, finally dead. He enjoyed the night time, the gunshots, the falling, the shuddering, the gargling, the holding on to life by a thread, and then the slow vanishing of life. It was like a melody to his ears, or a game. A game where he always won.

There was a submission in Daddy whenever we returned home together. It was as if he knew *what* he was. He could not cheat or bluff like he did with his friends, and with the stray dogs when he hid the shotgun behind his back and beckoned them closer as if he were offering them bread.

Daddy told Nisar and the old man once that he was asked to join the Dolphin Force, the esteemed police force that patrolled Lahore at night curbing crime, but he chose not to join because it was too much work. I knew that was a lie.

Outside the house, under the towering kikar, taali, and lemon trees of Victoria Colony, with the sly bats, sleepless strays, and effervescing shadows, Daddy unspooled. He was immortal.

The boy in Bungalow 17 was very special. Samander Khan, the driver, told me one day at work that Muhammad Daniyal was a miracle child like me.

I was a regular at the bungalow now. I cleaned cars, corridors, and the white kitchen counters upon the maid's commands. It was only after I cleaned that she permitted me to eat lunch in the kitchen. Otherwise, it was the driveway or the wet garden.

I was sitting on my haunches in the driveway, cleaning the muddy tires and bumper of the Land Cruiser with a water hose, when Khan told me the doctor had made the bungalow boy in a glass dish in a hospital.

I asked how that was even possible and how he knew. He said he drove madam and sir around to different clinics in Lahore and understood some English words when they conversed.

"Everything's possible in today's world, son," Samander Khan said. "Babies can be made in dishes. I saw a YouTube video on my mobile where an Indian doctor was telling how a baby's gender can be chosen. Men can get their *no-nos* cut and become girls."

I asked why my amma had to lose so many children and gain so much weight to have me if doctors could have done something.

"But for money. Everything can be bought from paisa." Samander Khan lifted the wiper blades and began cleaning the windshield of the Toyota. "And we're poor people. We get what we get. Boy. Girl. Stillborn. Nothing. This disease. That disease."

At that moment, the screen door on the porch flew open and the bungalow boy, Daniyal, hopped out with a cricket bat. It was time for us to play in the garden.

"300,000 rupees. That kid was made in three lakhs." Samander Khan jokingly winked. "We can buy fifty of you in that sum, Haider Ali."

Daniyal might have been a special child but now, like me, he was also lonely. Since I left school, I rarely had anyone to play with on the streets. In the mornings most of the children from the quarters left for school or their jobs, and in the afternoons and evenings when they played marbles or catch, I was either at the bungalow or out sweeping fallen leaves and juice boxes with Daddy.

Daniyal and I played for hours in the garden. Cricket, badminton, and video games on the big television set in his room. We peered at his colorful books with pictures of insects and fruit. He had a big bedroom full of toy cars, racetracks, stuffed animals, and every good thing I'd ever seen.

"What insects can we catch in the garden in November?" he asked, flipping through the book, running his index finger over the bright pages and big bold English words.

I placed my hand next to his on the picture of a winged insect. I noticed how dark my hand was compared to his.

"D . . . R . . . A . . . DRA . . . G . . . O . . . GON . . ." he mumbled the letters aloud as he tried to pronounce the insect's name. "Dragonfly!"

I told him I had seen many in the unkempt bushes near the servant quarters.

"Fireflies, butterflies, dragonflies," he said. "They're all in the summer. What can we catch at this time?"

I pretended to think along with him and flipped the glossy pages.

His daddy went to work in a new Toyota with an armed guard, while mine dove deep into gutters and shot dogs. His father taught him about fireflies and airplanes. Mine had begun asking me to scoop up the carcasses and put them in a cleanup truck.

Daniyal taught me how to write my name in English and count to twenty when we played hide-and-seek. I told him about my secret stray dog with a heart on its back and that Daniyal was a lucky boy that he didn't have a sister because I hated mine.

"Look at this." Daniyal showed me something in his book. It was a picture of a forest at night, lit up with tiny fireflies. They were like little balls of fire floating in the trees and plants. It was like when we had an open-fire stove in our quarters and Amma poked at the burning wood with tongs. Sparks would fly like the fireflies in the book.

"When my grandmother died last year," Daniyal said, "my daddy said her soul would leave her body and reach the heavens."

I wondered what that would look like. A soul leaving a body? I wanted to picture it in my head. Could I see the soul escaping up in the air when someone died?

"Maybe this is what happens when your father shoots a dog." Daniyal lay on the carpet, placed his hand under his chin, and flipped through the insect book. "The soul leaves the body like fireflies. Goes up and up and up like bright fireflies into the heavens."

One Sunday, Uncle Aslam and his wife with her pink lipstick, Neelam, took our family to the Bagh-e-Jinnah Park for a picnic.

Mother and Rashda sat on the Honda, carrying the picnic bindle while Daddy, Neelam, and I followed the laughing trio in a rickshaw my uncle paid for.

Daddy sulked and put on a clean gray shalwar-kameez for the occasion. He had disappeared behind the tree earlier for his mysterious ritual.

I could tell all morning, as we waited in the courtyard and watched Amma and Rashda prepare food, that Daddy was not looking forward to my uncle's picnic plan.

We sat on a dasterkhawan on the grass. Uncle Aslam showed off his new camera mobile. It had a huge screen and took clear pictures. Rashda posed for a few photos and asked my uncle if she could print them somehow because she had to show them to a friend.

Uncle Aslam told me if I returned to school, I could buy a similar phone. Maybe even an expensive one.

"What's the issue?" Uncle Aslam asked as we all sat down on the tablecloth to eat. "Why did you leave school, Haider Ali?"

"I . . . I . . ." I stammered, not knowing if I wanted to tell him the truth that I found the homework, the cramming of alphabets, words, the hours inside a classroom, and the blue uniform too dreary.

"Because he wasn't able to understand anything the teacher said," Rashda chimed in.

"That's not true," Daddy interjected. "He could've if he stayed. He's intelligent. It was his decision."

Uncle Aslam looked at my sister, then Daddy, and then back at me. "Is it true? Did you find your studies hard?"

"No," I lied. "I didn't. I understood everything in class."

"I can teach you if you want," Rashda offered.

I looked at her doubtfully, waiting for her to erupt in scornful laughter, but her face remained sincere.

"I know everything."

"Tell us the multiplication table of two," she challenged.

Daddy did not interfere the second time. Instead, he looked at me, like Mother did, like Neelam did, like Rashda and Uncle Aslam did. The pressure was serious.

"Two times two is . . ." I paused and looked at Daddy. I knew he wanted me to get it right for him, for us. "Eight?"

Rashda and Uncle Aslam shook their heads. Rashda laughed.

"I can count to twenty in English."

"School is not everything," Daddy finally said. "I found him a job. He'll be standing up on his feet in no time."

"Like you are? With your good job?" Amma said.

Daddy stopped eating after that. He gestured to me to rise and we left the picnic spot so he could smoke a cigarette by a tree.

"Does he still do nasha?" I heard my uncle ask my mother.

"He can sell us but he'll never leave drugs. There's rarely any money in the house now," my mother said. "There are complaints about him. Aslam, can you give me a thousand rupees for this week? I have to start asking our family for a loan."

Neelam made a face when Uncle Aslam took out a stylish blue wallet to help Amma out.

"I don't want Haider to quit school," I heard Rashda say. "I don't want him to become like *him*."

After the curry, parathas, roasted corn, and peanuts were devoured, and Neelam's pink lipstick was smudged around her mouth (which Uncle Aslam tenderly wiped with his handkerchief), we exited Bagh-e-Jinnah and crossed a busy road to get to where he had parked his motorbike. There was a rush of roaring traffic. Cars, rickshaws, motorbikes, and street vendors choked the narrow road.

Rashda froze in the middle of the moving traffic and placed hands over her ears like I did when Daddy shot dogs. A motorbike swerved, almost hitting her. The driver yelled, calling her mad and blind.

"That's a woman." Daddy snickered from the pavement.

We stood and watched Uncle Aslam raise his hand and motion a cackling rickshaw to come to a halt so he could rescue my petrified sister.

"All they can do is say vile things, but by the end of the day only a man can save them," Daddy said. "That's the reality of a woman. All words. Nothing more."

By January, I had fully immersed myself in my job at the bungalow. I'd also grown closer to Muhammad Daniyal.

We began sneaking out of the bungalow during afternoons after his mother had stopped bustling in and out of rooms and had retreated to her bedroom for a nap.

We met the black-and-white dog in the scaffoldings. He was a friend now. I had been saving him from my father for months by distracting or rerouting him during hunting nights.

"He doesn't bite," Daniyal often said.

"No, he doesn't."

"And he's so soft."
"So soft."
"There really is a heart on his back."
"There is."

With the frosty air and the blinding winter fog, a new feeling festered inside me. A new seed was sown. A seed of loathing. I began loathing the women in my house. Daddy spoke about Amma and Rashda with a relentless obsession. He said that he was a good pious teenager before he met Amma who performed black magic on him so she could command the house. It was because of her black magic that he was never in his senses, that he was now spending most of his hours sleeping in the park under trees. He should have married his cousin Nazia, his paternal uncle's pretty daughter.

"All women are churails," he told me now and then. "And these churails should be thrown in the canal."

"Even the madam in the bungalow? She's a witch too?"

"Even her."

"What about my old math teacher, Miss Farzana?"

"Her too. All of them."

I could agree about Rashda, Mother, and even Miss Farzana, who always held and twisted my ear in class and asked if I were paying attention, but my heart was not convinced that Daniyal's mother was a witch. She was too beautiful to be a churail. With her fair complexion, painted nails, and beautiful clothes, how could she be one? How could she be one if she asked me to scrub my feet before entering the living room because she did not like the carpets dirty?

Over the following wintry weeks, Daddy became nocturnal. He disappeared behind his tree a lot. There were days his breath was strangely pungent. I couldn't tell what he had eaten. He became raucous with his culling sprees, no longer restraining himself to Victoria Colony, his designated jurisdiction. There were barely any feral dogs left anyway. So Daddy strolled beyond it, terrorizing any creature he could find.

Sometimes he and I went to an adjacent neighborhood and bazaar in the middle of the night to shoot, when the clatter of the

city had died down and there were no witnesses. Once he shot a
sleeping cat under a chai stall. He said it was an accident.

"Pick it up," Daddy said when he shot a dog. "Toss it in that
rubbish pile over there."

*Over there. Over here. By that dumpster. By that sewer. In that
sewer. In that municipal truck. Just leave it there for other dogs.*

The bodies were always warm when I lifted them.

"You have to deposit the shotgun to the Colony administration
soon," Samander Khan informed Daddy one morning when he
and I were hosing down the driveway. The driver watched us and
cleaned his ear with the key of the Toyota.

"Why?"

"They'll begin poisoning the dogs from now on," he said.
"Strychnine in chicken meat. Only the security guards will keep
their guns."

I could see Daddy's face wilt and wither as if he were a little boy
and someone was taking away his favorite toy.

"We'll see," Daddy said. "I didn't hear any orders yet."

"There aren't any dogs left anyway. What will you shoot, sahib
ji?"

The two men kept talking. My mind drifted somewhere else,
to my own black-and-white dog. How would I save him from
poisoned chicken?

"Bad day for you," Samander Khan guffawed at Daddy. "Good
day for Nisar Khan, the butcher."

With Daddy barely bringing his salary home, there was always
a downpour at home. As the months crawled by, Amma had
frequent meltdowns. Rashda had not paid her school or evening
tuition fees in two months. Like Amma, Rashda often told Daddy
to mend his ways. She did not want to leave her education and
work at a call center like her friend Bushra.

Amma announced that the sir and madam from Bungalow 17
had called her to say they no longer wanted Daddy in the house
because of his suspicious habits. They were willing to keep me as
an errand boy and Amma as a new maid, but they did not want my
father entering the threshold.

It was not just the hunting privileges Daddy was losing, but his job at the bungalow. He had to do other odd jobs to make ends meet.

Amma also said I was not allowed in the kitchen either.

"Or their son's bedroom or any other rooms in the house," she said.

I smelled of cigarettes and other bad things. The family said I smelled like Daddy.

One evening Amma hollered, wailed, broke two ceramic plates on the kitchen floor, hit her head with her hands in the courtyard, beat her chest, and berated Daddy after she found a white powder and syringe in Daddy's kameez when she was doing laundry.

Amma held him by the collar and asked why he was hell-bent on ruining her life. Daddy pushed her back. She did not fall. I wanted her to. Amma stood steadfast.

Daddy's response was that the cleric at the mosque told him it was the wife who brought good luck and sustenance in a marriage, and that it was Amma who was the manhoos one.

The doomed, unlucky one.

Amma kept spewing curses. Daddy kept spewing them back. I felt I had a duty toward him.

"Leave him alone," I shouted at Amma. "If you want more money, go work yourself. Are your arms and legs broken?"

Mother stood, mortified. After finally fathoming my words, she said in a strained voice, "For two years, I didn't eat lentils because the big pir from Multan told me not to. For years, I prayed for a son. I shouldn't have if I knew this is what he'd become."

"You shouldn't have prayed then. You should've strangled me so you could live peacefully with your churail daughter."

Amma did not reply with an "I wish I had."

"Do you see how the witches are conspiring against us?" Daddy said to me one night. "I wish I had more sons who would stand up for their old father."

"Why did Daniyal's daddy kick you out?"

"Because he is an emasculated son-of-a-bitch who is controlled by his woman. He does whatever the madam says."

I reflected and remained quiet.

"How else can a man who is always at the office, never at home, suddenly kick me out of the job?"

There were many other questions I wanted to ask Daddy. Like why did he smoke so much? *Smoking kills.* Daniyal had taught me that phrase. Why did Daddy need an injection? Was he sick? How sick was he? Why couldn't Daddy take a computer course like Uncle Aslam and get a new job? And a Honda?

Daddy turned to look at me when I didn't respond with affirmation. I knew what he was thinking—I was siding with my mother and betraying him. Before he rebuked me with his favorite lines—*Why don't you cut your penis and become like Uncle Aslam?*—my tongue thawed and I said, "Why don't we get Rashda married?"

"Marry off your sister?" Daddy replied. "This way, she'll be out of the house. Less chitter-chatter. Less drama. Now you're thinking like a man."

In the next few days, Daddy was able to convince Amma that my sister would have a better life if she got married to Rehan. She could still sit for her board exams, keep taking science tuitions, and pay for her daily rickshaw rides. It was our cousin's family who would be responsible for her monthly expenditures. Not us. They were better off than we were.

"It's within the family," Daddy said. "What can go wrong? She had to marry after matric anyway, why not a few months earlier? And if you talk to baji in Bungalow 17, she will help with the dowry."

Amma thought about it.

"We can have a little ceremony. I know a man who can add a string of lights outside," he continued. "I know another man who can put a tent outside for a few guests."

Amma thought some more.

"My dead grandfather gave my brother his word. We can't break it."

My sister felt deceived by our mother. She felt Amma was selling her to a man similar to Daddy.

"Why can't I marry a learned man?" she said when the news was broken to her. "Why can't I marry someone else after matric? A man of my choosing."

"You've been promised. We gave them our word," Amma said. "If we turn our back on the family, they'll all turn their backs on us. It's also the family reputation in the village."

Rashda argued some more, but deep down, she knew there was no way out. There had never been a way out for other unhappy family members who wanted to break their arranged betrothals. She became morbidly quiet after that decision.

There were times when I tried to engage with her since I had never seen her so somber, stewing in silence. I did not enjoy it like I thought I would, but Daddy did. Daddy was very happy. After a while, Amma also became happy once the madam gave her 50,000 rupees in cash for the dowry. Uncle Aslam was happy to learn we'd found a way for Rashda to pass her matriculation.

I had my own worries. I was dejected by my separation from Daniyal. I was limited to cleaning corridors, the garden, the driveway. The maid had started bringing her son to the bungalow for Daniyal to play with sometimes.

Her son went to school and did not smell of cigarettes.

A week before the wedding, and a few days before Rehan's family and other relatives were to arrive in Lahore from Hafizabad, Rashda went missing. Her charpoy was empty. Her school bag and a few clothes were also missing.

Amma and I looked everywhere. Around the servant quarters. Around Victoria Colony. After a while, we began looking for Daddy. After failing at that too, we resumed the first search. We took a rickshaw to Rashda's school, the tuition center, and her friend Bushra's house. My sister was nowhere.

Around noon, two police constables arrived at our house in a rackety charcoal-gray pickup with blue and red lights on top. They had found a dead, bloody body of a young girl on Canal Road, not far from Victoria Colony. She was hit by a car while attempting to cross the wide road in the middle of the night. The streetlamps were not working due to a short circuit.

They had found her name scribbled on the first page of her school diary, where she had also written down Uncle Aslam's new mobile number. He had identified the body at the morgue.

Mother did not cry. She did not shriek. She howled. It was a guttural howl like that of a wounded animal. Like one that a dog made when Daddy shot it only in the leg. Her cry pierced through my skin, penetrated my bones, wrecked something in my heart.

My body went numb. Amma howled again. And again. And again. I wanted to stop her pain. I wanted to strangle Amma to soothe her pain, and then go hunting for Daddy.

Uncle Aslam and I did not speak much as our motorbike followed the blaring Edhi ambulance home. My sister was inside that car. I held on to her school bag and clothes as my uncle zoomed through Lahore traffic. We took the same Canal Road home. And the same 50,000 rupees that Daniyal's mother handed Amma were to be used on the funeral instead.

As Uncle Aslam and I halted at a red light, I watched the white ambulance with yellow and red markings. I thought I saw hundreds of little fireflies pouring through the car doors, windows, taillights, and the exhaust pipe. Escaping. Soaring. Floating in the dusty, dirty, murky air. Up. Up. Into the heavens.

The night after the burial, Daddy went haunting the dogs again. Reeling out of control again. I followed him.

Daddy's mourning was different than Amma's. He swung the shotgun after the mourners left and after my sister was buried in the small colony graveyard, and he shot everything that night. He told me that he would shoot everything before *they* could take away his gun.

He shot chickens.

Rats.

His kikar tree.

Inside a gutter.

An old discarded glass table in the garbage pile. It shattered everywhere.

Daddy and I reached the scaffolding near Bungalow 17. A lightbulb hung at the construction site illuminating only a small area. Everything else rested in shadows.

I knew my black-and-white dog would not be there. I had not seen it in a while. I expected it to be poisoned and dumped somewhere by now. A part of me was glad I didn't have to see its dead body. I was still unable to erase my sister from my mind. Rashda's body had been draped in a white shroud, and then we had carried it to the graveyard and slowly suspended it down a freshly dug grave. I had placed a mound of dirt on her body.

I tried to trick Daddy into leaving the scaffolding. I could not see another dead body that day. I told him there was a security guard manning the construction site.

Daddy kept moving forward.

"The security guard has a gun," I said.

Daddy stumbled over a brick, regained his balance, and continued walking.

"Did you hear something?" he asked.

Just then, my black-and-white dog emerged at a distance from behind a plastic tarp. It was frailer than before. I heaved a sigh of relief to see it was alive and breathing.

The dog wagged his tail, recognizing me, but whined and moved back when he saw Daddy with the shotgun.

"Here." Daddy handed me the gun. "You're a man now. Shoot. See how it feels."

I locked eyes with Daddy. His eyes were tinged with red.

"No."

He loaded the barrel of the shotgun and shoved the gun into my arms again.

"No Daddy. Don't." I shook my head violently. "We can't."

Daddy pushed me away and aimed for the dog. I tugged at Daddy's arm, wrestling him for the gun. He pushed me away with a great force and I fell on the ground. Daddy aimed the shotgun at me. I did not cower or raise my hands to surrender like I had seen in movies with Muhammad Daniyal.

I looked straight at Daddy. I looked into his eyes. There was nothing there. Nothing. There was no splinter of emotion in Daddy's eyes.

Daddy chuckled, shaking his head, delighted that he had frightened me. He turned the shotgun toward the dog. I looked away. I did not cover my ears. There was a loud ringing in my ears from the gunshot.

From the corner of my eye, I saw something move.

Fireflies. Thousands of them. Glowing. Gliding. Hovering above the black-and-white dog's body. Wafting through the old ghostly trees. Up. Up. Away from Victoria Colony. Away from Daddy.

I walked home in silence, leaving my father by himself.

When Daddy returned home eventually, he told me he shot many other things after I left him.

I squatted on the floor and looked up at Daddy who was sitting on the charpoy in the courtyard, cleaning the shotgun with a rag. He said he was ready to return it tomorrow.

I wanted the gun to go off, for one of the slugs to ricochet and kill Daddy. He broke my heart. He broke Amma's heart. He broke Rashda.

"Sister-fucker," I whispered.

"What did you say?"

"If someone kills you and throws your body in a gutter," I said. "No one will come looking for you. No one will miss you, Daddy."

I said he was a stray, feral, useless thing no one wanted.

"Haraam khor," Daddy abused me, enraged. "Unfaithful. Coward."

"I don't want to be like you."

"Haraam khor."

Haraam khor. Haraam khor.

Daddy kept chanting as I left him in the courtyard.

A WOMAN'S COLLEGE GIRL IN A LIBRARY

Emily Herring Wilson

Suddenly, they took our name and put men in our beds,
Registered cars and built large parking towers.
Then the various boards, trustees, and committees thanked
Themselves for being such careful stewards of their power.
We had been taught that service was our mission.
Modesty is so yesterday; let's be outstanding.
Read the Official Rulebook of Branding.
Wipe us out, quick, take down Virginia Dare, wanna?
Who heard of her or someone named Tatyana?
Only a poet with a reader's knowledge.
They don't get it, do they? Love is what made Woman's College.

The Robert Watson Literary Prize Poem
THEORY WHEN A WESTERN LIGHT GOES OUT

L.A. Johnson

Tonight, the wind plucks leaves from their branches.
A coroner, it drops

the near-dead
in front of my door. I rise to the porch, gather the halfway

bodies. Pressed between dictionary pages, their veins
leave brown stains

like blood.
Little souls stamped between *faucet* and *fog, dead* and *dreaming,*

alive and *alone.* I hang their imprints on the wall.
As a girl, I played

a silver harmonica
that I swore would sound without a mouth to it,

a wind made by those mouths locked in meadows,
their teeth gone.

Once, I saw a stag
set to be buried in a coffin, satin-lined. His antlers sleeked,

his muscles glistened slick with embalming fluid.
Even then I thought

how strong—
the animal poised to leap in a different life.

In a different life, the invisible would not just be visible
but more beautiful.

Every past
wrong, undone: the stag not dead, but awake

in a green meadow; a hole in the ceiling not for a leak
but for rain,

warm rain,
to clean the interior; my father, not buried

but sleeping
the peaceful sleep of a body in love with the earth.

HOW WE DEVEIN DISTANCE
Alyx Chandler

Another year at the open bar
slathered in melted butter—

this is how the Gulf peels back
my family: like a thin knife

along shrimp entrails—
a quick *slit* then lift. We

pinch tails with teeth, toast
to a messy-eat. What's abundance

more like than laughter,
a soft spot for how

what couldn't heal
suddenly can in the sunlight.

I find forgiveness
where I least expect it:

wild-caught in the
alimentary canal,

that gull-release of nerve
in warm, briny air—

relatives torn open tableside
in the cocktail of sincerity,

savoring what's left
of each other, what we

haven't yet devoured.

NOTES ON CONTRIBUTORS

NICOLE ADABUNU's poetry has been published in *Writer's Digest.* Currently, she is a poetry MFA candidate at the Iowa Writers' Workshop as an Iowa Arts Fellow and lives in Iowa City, Iowa.

MOLLY GUINN BRADLEY's work has appeared in *Bon Appétit, Electric Literature, Joyland Magazine,* and *The Toast.* She is a writer and editor in Brooklyn, New York.

ALYX CHANDLER's poetry can be found in *Cordella Magazine* and *Glass House Press.* Currently, she serves in the AmeriCorps VISTA for two Montana creative writing nonprofits as well as being a publicist for *Poetry Northwest* and a reader for *Electric Literature.*

EMILY CINQUEMANI has work in *32 Poems, Colorado Review, Indiana Review, Nashville Review,* and *Ploughshares,* among others. She teaches at the South Carolina Governor's School for the Arts and Humanities in Greenville, South Carolina.

KEVIN MCWILLIAMS COATES currently works as an instructional coach and teacher trainer after retiring from elementary school teaching. She lives in San Rafael, California.

NATALIA CONTE has been published in *Pedestal Magazine, So to Speak, SWWIM,* and others. She lives in New York City. You can find her work at nataliaconte.com.

JULIA EDWARDS has work in *Bat City Review, Diode,* and *Poetry Magazine,* among others. She is currently a visiting poet in the Working Poets Project at The Dalton School. She lives in Brooklyn, New York.

JEREMY HALINEN's poetry collection *What Other Choice* won the 2010 Exquisite Disarray First Book Poetry Contest. His poems have appeared in journals including *Cimarron Review, Court Green, The Los Angeles Review, Poet Lore,* and *Sentence,* and in anthologies including *Best Gay Poetry 2008* and *I Go to the Ruined Place: Contemporary Poems in Defense of Global Human Rights.*

KANZA JAVED is the author of the novel *Ashes, Wine and Dust.* Her work has been published in *American Literary Review, The Punch Magazine,* and *Salamander.* Her short story, "Ran," won the 2020 Reynolds Price Prize for Fiction.

L.A. JOHNSON is the author of the chapbook *Little Climates.* Her poems have recently appeared or are forthcoming in *The American Poetry Review, Poetry Magazine, The Rumpus, The Southern Review, ZYZZYVA,* and other journals. The winner of the 2021 Rumi Prize in Poetry, she was named a Gregory Djanikian Scholar by the *Adroit Journal.* Find her online at la-johnson.com.

PETER KENT has published poems in *Cimarron Review, Lullwater Review, New Millennium Writings, The Opiate, Sixfold,* and other journals. He lives in Boston, Massachusetts.

ROBERT WOOD LYNN'S debut collection of poetry, *Mothman Apologia,* was selected by Rae Armantrout as the 2021 winner of the Yale Series of Younger Poets Prize and is forthcoming in April 2022 from Yale University Press. His work has appeard in *The Cincinnati Review, Michigan Quarterly Review, Narrative Magazine, Shenandoah,* and other journals. He splits his time between New York City and Rockbridge County, Virginia.

MATT W. MILLER is the author of the poetry collections *Tender the River, The Wounded for the Water, Club Icarus,* selected by Major Jackson as the winner of the 2012 Vassar Miller Poetry Prize, and *Cameo Diner: Poems.* A former Wallace Stegner Fellow in Poetry at Stanford University and a Walter E. Dakin Fellow in Poetry at the Sewanee Writers' Conference, he teaches at Phillips Exeter Academy and lives with his family in coastal New Hampshire.

JED MYERS is the author of the poetry collections *Watching the Perseids* and *The Marriage of Space and Time*, and four chapbooks, including *Dark's Channels* and *Love's Test*. His poems can be found in *The American Journal of Poetry, Poetry Northwest, Prairie Schooner, Rattle*, and elsewhere. He is the Poetry Editor for *Bracken* and lives in Seattle, Washington.

ELLEN RHUDY'S fiction has appeared in *The Cincinnati Review, Cream City Review, Split Lip*, and *Story*, among others. A former Peace Corps volunteer and Fulbright grantee, she is now an MFA candidate at The Ohio State University and lives in Columbus, Ohio.

K.R. SEGRIFF'S work has appeared in *PRISM International, Riddle Fence*, and *Storm Cellar*, among others, and her short films have been selected for over fifty film festivals worldwide. She is a Canadian writer, filmmaker, and visual artist.

AKSHAY SHRIVASTAVA'S work has appeared in *The Threepenny Review*. He is a data scientist and lives in Chicago, Illinois.

MELISSA STUDDARD is the author of two poetry collections, *I Ate the Cosmos for Breakfast* and *Dear Selection Committee*, and the chapbook *Like a Bird with a Thousand Wings*. Her work has been featured by *The New York Times*, *NPR*, and the *Academy of American Poets*' Poem-a-Day series, and has appeared in periodicals such as *Harvard Review, Kenyon Review, New England Review*, and *POETRY,* among others.

CLANCY TRIPP'S work has appeared in or is forthcoming from *Black Warrior Review, Catapult, Electric Literature, The Florida Review*, and *Ninth Letter*. She is a Midwest-based writer, graphic artist, and humorist. Find her on Twitter @TheUnrealTripp or at ClancyTripp.com.

EMILY HERRING WILSON is the author of numerous books of nonfiction, most recently *The Three Graces of Val-Kill: Eleanor*

Roosevelt and Her Friends. Her work has been recognized with fellowships from the National Endowment for the Humanities, the North Carolina Arts Council, and the MacDowell Colony as well as the Mayfield Award for North Carolina Women and the North Carolina Award, the highest civilian honor given by the state. She lives in Winston-Salem, North Carolina.

The Greensboro Review
would like to thank the following supporters
for their generous contributions

Heather Adams

Dan Albergotti

Lynne Barrett

Fred & Susan Chappell

Steve Cushman

Michael & Emily Cinquemani

Whitney Collins

Matthew Fiander

Nathan Golden

Zac Goldstein

Coppie Green

Brandon Haffner

Robin Hendricks

David Hough

Kristen Inciardi

Matthew Johnson

Ken Joyner

Christina Louvet

Robert Lynn

Jeff Martin

Valerie Nieman

Sophie Nunberg

Jon Obermeyer

David Roderick

George Singleton

Chris Swensen

Betty Watson

Jim Whiteside

If you would like to find out how you can contribute
to *The Greensboro Review* endowment
and keep us in print
please contact Jeff Sapp
336-334-3443
jmsapp@uncg.edu

Subscribe

The Greensboro Review is published twice yearly, in the fall and spring. You can subscribe online through the University of North Carolina Press.

Rates:

Individuals
$14.00 per year
$24.00 for two years
$30.00 for three years

Institutions
$16.00 per year
$28.00 for two years

For international orders, additional shipping rates will added when you purchase a subscription

UNC Press has a new partnership with Duke University Press (DUP) for handling print subscriptions for *The Greensboro Review*. Agencies are eligible for a discount on the institutional rate. If you have questions about an existing subscription please contact DUP Journal Services:

- Individuals can order online at https://uncpjournals.dukeupress.edu/the-greensboro-review
- Email subscriptions@dukeupress.edu
- Phone toll-free in the US and Canada (888) 651-0122
- Phone (919) 688-5134